WHERE *Starlight* BURNS

A Novel

Alicia Haberski

First published by Kosmic Syren Books 2023

Copyright © 2023 by Alicia Haberski

All rights reserved. No part of this publication may be reproduced, stored or transmitted in any form or by any means, electronic, mechanical, photocopying, recording, scanning, or otherwise without written permission from the publisher. It is illegal to copy this book, post it to a website, or distribute it by any other means without permission.

This novel is entirely a work of fiction. The names, characters and incidents portrayed in it are the work of the author's imagination. Any resemblance to actual persons, living or dead, events or localities is entirely coincidental.

First edition

Copyedited by Lauren Humphries-Brooks

Proofread by Elizabeth Thurmond

Cover design by Alicia Haberski

Cover art by Luminas_Art and interozitor via Pixabay

ISBN 979-8-9884978-1-3

For all the other nerdy gals who love to dream about the future. Let's never stop.

Contents

Victory   1
Secrets   17
Parasite   31
The Truth   45
Scars   59
Love Songs   75
Oasis   91
Perspective   103
Wounds   115
To the Stars   125
Ascension   135
Little Eden   151
Zion   167
Remember Earth   179
The Beach   197
Safety   207
Centauride   223
Vows   245
Home   259
New Life   273
Starlight   285

Acknowledgments   297
About the Author   299

1
Victory

Few people in the galaxy traveled to Victory Station on purpose. Among those who did, even fewer were *excited* about the trip. And fewer still planned to stay longer than a day or two, on a pit stop during a longer journey to a (hopefully) more pleasant place.

But as Dr. Corinth "Cori" Nova stepped inside Victory for the first time, she saw things differently. This station, with its rusting poles and crowded footpaths, would be her new home. With it came a new beginning. Stepping across the threshold between the transit port and the forked pathway that offered multiple gates toward the interior, she took a moment to privately celebrate her arrival at this odd city floating in space. The oldest human-made station still operational, in fact, and the type of place she could have only dreamed of seeing in her youth.

Continuing across a bridge leading from the docks to a residential sector, the air took on a noticeably moldy, metallic smell. Looking down, she had a view of the engineering level below, with so many well-worn machines clanking and groaning as operators dutifully kept the station running.

As she neared the edge of the neighborhood, or "zone," she was approaching, she stopped again, just to take it all in: stacked apartments with staircases warped from decades of use, flanked by a long street crowded with foot traffic and a motorized hauler beeping in the distance.

To Cori, the dilapidated structures only added to the unique beauty of this place—full of so many people, from all corners of the galaxy, peacefully coexisting. And, perhaps, united on a single issue: distaste for the station itself.

"Yep, still reeks," came a voice somewhere in the crowd.

Then someone else collided with Cori from behind with surprising force. She turned to see them scrambling to pick up two dropped bags and stooped to help.

"Fucking stars," the person—shorter than her and with bright green hair—muttered, snatching the second bag from Cori's hand. "Are you really just *standing* there?"

They went their separate ways. Cori continued on to find her new apartment and drop off her luggage. It was a simple complex on another residential block, where there were plenty of openings, and her single-bedroom unit had a charming lounge area and a window that overlooked the road below. It would suit her needs perfectly.

Afterward, Cori set out to her second destination: clinic 4H. She could take a train, which would zip her there in minutes, but she decided to make the walk—she wanted to see more of Victory. She attempted to connect to the station's network via her neural implant, but all she got were error messages informing her the system was down. She had a hunch it had been that way for some time. No matter; the map she'd previously downloaded was sufficient.

The way there turned out to be a master class of sights, sounds, and smells, as she cut a path through a busy square where people were rushing in every direction, and onto an elevator that would take her down a few levels. Now that she had traveled beyond the human residential zone, there was a mixture of species: She passed a pair of fluffy Irsids waking together and then a tentacled Crindorian, hurrying somewhere on robotic legs. As she stepped inside the elevator, she knew it must be strange for her to be smiling so much—the other passengers were grimacing at an especially potent odor—but she found it impossible to stop.

When she arrived at the clinic, with its large clear doors, she went straight to the reception desk. A nurse scanned her wrist chip.

"Dr. Nova, welcome," the nurse said. "The director is waiting for you just down the hall, if you'll follow me."

As they walked, Cori took stock of the clinic, pleased that it was clean and well-kept, despite being the smallest one on the station and in a somewhat removed location. She would be proud to serve as head physician here, for the first time in her career.

The nurse showed Cori to a small office, where she met Dr. Arthur Davis, the director of human health, who oversaw all four human clinics on the station. He might have been imposing once with his broad stature, Cori reflected, but his weary expression and tired posture softened the edges a bit.

"I wanted to come down and personally meet you," Dr. Davis explained, "and find out if there's anything you need from me. I understand this is all new to you."

"That's right. I appreciate it, but I think I'm all set. I'm eager to get started."

Dr. Davis raised his eyebrows. "Hopefully this station won't dull your energy ... To be honest, I'm surprised you're here. Actually. Ah, heck. Can I ask you a personal question?"

"Of course."

"*Why* are you here? I mean, don't get me wrong, we're very glad to have you. But you're way overqualified with all those recommendations ... You must have had plenty of options back in the major worlds. Why did you choose to come out to Victory?"

Cori took a moment to consider the question. She did have several offers lined up now that she had completed her residency at a hospital on Idun. She could have easily stayed there or hopped to some other planet and found a cozy practice and a fancy apartment with a nice view. But she craved a real adventure—she'd long imagined traveling through the stars, making a home in space, and getting to see how people lived out here.

"It seemed like a place where I could do a lot of good," she responded. "I want to help as many people as possible. But that's what we all want, isn't it?"

"Absolutely," he agreed, with the same quick eyebrow raise. "Well, it's good to meet you. And again, thank you for swooping in and saving my ass. I thought this position might take months to fill; I wasn't sure how we'd keep the clinic operating in the meantime."

Cori was taken aback. "In that case, I'm *sure* I made the right decision."

After the meeting, Cori changed into her new uniform, constructed of white fabric and plain compared to what she had worn previously, but practical and sturdy. There was no need for a doctor's attire to be anything else, anyway.

Her first shift in the new role brought in an array of patients: the child who crashed a motorbike and cracked a fibula, the elderly person with joint pain, the shopkeeper with an odd cough, and many more. Most of the patients assigned to this clinic were long-term residents of the same zone where Cori's new apartment was located. As they came and went, she started to get a feel for the way they lived and worked.

The last patient of her shift turned out to be the most memorable.

Cori stepped into the exam room, having been advised of a wrist fracture and preparing for a swift and straightforward healing, when she stopped short at the sight of the patient before her: Aster Moss, a woman in her late twenties with the most stunning auburn hair Cori had ever seen—half swept up and half flowing over her shoulders in dark red waves. She was tall and thin, like many spacers, with light eyes and sharp features, and her skin was fair enough that dark bruises on her face and left arm stood in stark contrast. Her right arm was covered in artwork, fully visible thanks to her sleeveless top.

"Hello," Cori started, stepping closer. "I'm Dr. Nova. You're Aster, correct?"

Aster nodded, eyes a bit glassy and tired. "It's just my wrist."

"Ah," Cori said with a nod. "Let me take a look."

Using her tablet scanner, Cori took a quick render of the bones in Aster's wrist and hand, where she zoomed in on the fracture and then rotated it.

"Oof," she remarked. "Bet that didn't feel good. But fortunately, it's an easy fix. I'll just get you some meds for the pain first."

"Oh, no," Aster said nervously. "I can't have those. The meds, I mean."

"Oh? Do you have an allergy?"

There were no warnings in Aster's chart about specific meds, so Cori wanted to be sure to add one if needed.

"No," Aster replied, glancing down, her voice small. "Not exactly."

"Okay," Cori responded, not wanting to press too hard. "Well, I'm sorry to say the procedure is highly unpleasant without them. If you change your mind, just let me know."

That got her a quick nod.

Cori prepared the cellular repair and regeneration device, commonly known as a healing lamp, calibrating it to the correct tissue and level of injury, then holding it over Aster's wrist.

"Just keep your arm still and relaxed and the healing lamp will do the rest. If you do move, it may need recalibration, but that's not a problem."

Aster nodded again. "Thank you."

This machine was an older model than the ones Cori had trained with, but it functioned the same, detecting the limb and automatically adjusting to its size, prongs emerging and gently affixing to the arm before the status light blinked orange and the progress meter began at zero percent. As it worked, it cast a purple glow on the skin, illuminating the section of the body being repaired.

Given Aster's refusal of pain meds and the fact that no other patients were currently waiting, Cori decided it would be best to keep her company. She pulled over a chair and sat beside the bed, a bit surprised that Aster hadn't reacted to the treatment at all.

A tattoo of a bird on Aster's shoulder caught Cori's eye,

as it suddenly flapped its wings twice before going still again. Below it, a flowering vine encircled her bicep, and lower still, there was an asterism, and so on, all the way down her arm.

"What incredible work," Cori said. "And such an interesting collection."

"Oh, thanks," Aster said, "I like to get one for every station I visit."

"Stars above!" Cori said, fighting disbelief. "That's so many! What an adventurous life. I admire that."

For the first time, Aster smiled. "How long have you been here, on Victory?"

"I just arrived today, actually."

"My condolences."

Cori laughed. "Would you believe it's my *first time* on a station at all?"

Aster's eyes went wide at that, and then the healing lamp beeped to signal completion, the status light now green. Cori removed it from her wrist and set it aside before rescanning the area. "Beautiful!" she said, finding the bone good as new. "Well, Aster, is there anything else I can do for you today?"

She shook her head.

"Then I wish you safe travels. I'm very glad to have met you. Oh!" Cori turned to open one of the cabinets in the room, scanning her chip for access and then retrieving a small tube of ointment. "Take this for the bruising. It'll speed up the healing and numb the tenderness. It's mild enough that you can't overuse it."

Aster gave her an odd look but accepted the tube. "Thanks. It was... nice to meet you, too."

That night, back in her apartment, Cori thought about the patients she had met on her first day as head physician. She was optimistic about this new chapter of her life. No two days would be the same on Victory, and that was part of the appeal: the endless stream of fascinating individuals living their lives, who just needed to be patched up now and then so they could get back to what really mattered.

Her thoughts drifted to Aster, someone with whom Cori would never have crossed paths had she not decided to come here. In fact, had she not arrived today, they might have missed each other completely.

A small part of her hoped to see Aster again sometime, for reasons she couldn't articulate, but she shook off the thought—it was far more sensible to hope that Aster would stay healthy, and that she'd be on her way soon to a place where she could have more fun.

Only four days later, however, Cori's wish came true: Aster was back in the clinic.

Cori did a double take when she saw the ID and status

on her tablet—not only for the familiar name, but for the worst injury she had seen all day: two fractured ribs.

Hurrying into the room, she found Aster in far worse condition than last time. She was lying on the bed with her arms around her torso, drawing in ragged breaths and whining from the pain.

"Oh no, you poor thing! Let me take a look. Can you raise your arms away from your side for me?"

Aster did as instructed. As Cori gently lifted her shirt, she was shocked by the extent of dark bruising around the injury site. It appeared to be several hours old, and she wondered why Aster would wait so long to come in, but that wasn't the only oddity: across her torso were rows of other, smaller bruises in nearly perfect circles. Cori had never seen anything like that, but her first priority was the rib injury.

After a fresh scan confirmed the dual fracture, Cori reached for an adhesive analgesic sheet—having personally ordered some after Aster's last appointment, to be better prepared for similar scenarios.

"This is for pain relief," she explained. "Let's get you more comfortable."

"No," Aster said, shaking her head, brow furrowed. "I can't have that."

"This one is perfectly safe."

Aster shook her head again. "It's against the rules."

"What?" Cori asked, bewildered. "What *rules?*"

"Didn't they tell you?" Aster asked through her teeth, frustrated. "Escorts can't *have* pain meds."

"Is that the only reason you've refused twice now?"

At Aster's nod, Cori discarded the adhesive and took up a syringe of the much more effective universal pain med.

"We'll, I've never heard of that rule, so with your consent, I'd like to give you two doses of AnoDyn, as your condition clearly warrants."

Aster's brow was furrowed. "I don't want to get you in any trouble. Dr. Rylen would never let me have any . . . It's too wasteful."

Cori disguised the disgust and rage she felt at that information.

"Listen. You're my patient now. I don't care what Dr. Rylen told you, and I have no intention of ever following such a rule, as it goes against every ethical principle I uphold. With your consent, I'll give you a double dose of AnoDyn, and we'll both feel much better."

At that, Aster nodded, eyes glistening a bit. "Okay."

Using the syringe, Cori took Aster's arm and stamped her skin twice, releasing the drug into her system and watching as the tension melted away—relaxing her posture and her brow.

"Thank you," Aster said, breathing more easily. "I really hope you don't get any shit for that."

"I forbid you from worrying about me," Cori said. "Just relax while I get you patched up. You're going to be fine."

The treatment for the broken ribs took longer than the previous injury, but thanks to the medication, Aster was able to fall asleep as the healing lamp went to work. While she was out, Cori took some time to go over her medical file. Though she found no notes about her profession nor any imposed limitations on treatments, there was a "status" indicator she hadn't noticed before: *Low Priority.*

Stepping into the hallway, Cori spotted a nurse and asked what time Aster had arrived for treatment.

"This morning, as usual," came the clipped answer.

Cori's heart sank to think of Aster waiting all day for treatment with such a painful injury. "Could you explain what you mean?"

The nurse, an older woman named Elynor, seemed to remember herself, straightening her back and answering more professionally. "This patient has been a regular for a while, Dr. Nova. She's a prostitute—I mean, literally. Not at the pleasure center, but out on the streets."

"She's doing sex work off the record?" Cori asked.

"Not just that," Elynor said, stepping closer so she could lower her voice. "She's out there escorting *other species*. They're the ones who pay for that around here. It's very much off the record. No regulations. No documentation. Nothing. They can just…do whatever they want with her." She punctuated the description with a silent gag.

"And is it true that Dr. Rylen didn't administer pain meds for her?"

Elynor nodded. "He said it was our responsibility not to encourage her... He was a good doctor, but he was set in his ways, you know? Honestly, I thought she'd have given up by now. Guess all that money is worth it."

"Thank you for explaining," Cori said. "Could you send me her appointment log, please?"

When the list arrived on her tablet moments later, Cori was stunned to see that it dated back more than a year—and that she was looking at dozens of appointments for minor to moderate injuries.

As the pieces fell into place, Cori gained a clearer picture of this patient and her relationship with the clinic. Cori had studied enough about galactic society to know that there were all sorts of "semi-legal" lines of work: that is, dangerous occupations not formally sanctioned, offered no contracts or protections, but not outright banned. This type of prostitution, however, was widely regarded as unethical at best and repulsive at worst. Elynor was hardly unique in finding it distasteful. Anyone engaged in the practice was perceived to be sullying the reputation not only of sex workers, but of all humans, by allowing other species to treat them like "toys" after humans had spent decades fighting for more respect in the galaxy.

Cori had always found it unimaginable that anyone would willingly choose that line of work when so many other avenues existed. And yet, here was Aster, a real human being who was actively enduring it. At once, Cori realized that the round bruises could have come from famously strong Crindorian tentacles—and if that were the case, Aster was fortunate that her injury wasn't *worse*.

That thought brought up only sympathy. Cori simply refused to judge this patient in any way due to a situation she couldn't possibly understand, perhaps out of personal intuition as much as doctoral ethics. What did trouble her, however, was the knowledge that the previous doctor in her own position had repeatedly withheld pain medication for an injured patient. What inexcusable sadism and a gross abuse of power. Any doctor who *punished* their patients was no true healer at all. Not only had he made Aster's appointments a source of misery, he had risked pushing her toward dangerous alternatives—used without proper training and calibration, healing lamps could easily grow tumors or cause other horrendous complications.

Cori had never been one to believe in fate, but she appreciated the concept of it. And if anything like fate did exist in the universe, then it had to be her fate to end up right here. She switched Aster's status to *High Priority* and closed the file.

Back in Aster's room, Cori took a full torso scan, just to be sure there were no additional injuries. Her intuition was correct: All the other bruises were superficial, consistent with suction cups.

Aster was awake when Cori removed the healing lamp and rescanned her ribs.

"Beautiful. I've set out some more bruise salve for you here when you're ready to go, but you're welcome to rest a while. Is there anything else I can do for you today?"

Aster shook her head. "I feel a lot better than I have in a long time. Thanks for your help."

"You're very welcome. Be careful out there."

After they parted ways once again, Cori was oddly happy to think that Aster would be a regular patient. But perhaps it wasn't strange at all to be glad that she could be her doctor, now, and give her the proper unbiased care she deserved all along.

2

Secrets

Aster was lying in a musty motel bed, laughing so hard that tears were streaming down her temples.

Her left foot was in the large mouth of an Irsid—human sweat tasted like ambrosia to them, apparently—and instead of a tongue and teeth, their species had soft barbels lining the inside of their mouths, which meant that this fucking *tickled*.

The first few times she'd experienced it, she'd done her best to hold the laughs in, but eventually she'd learned that the clients were too preoccupied to care.

Just then, an alarm chimed on her comm.

"That's time," she said in between laughs. "Hour's up."

They withdrew slightly but lingered on her toes.

"Hey," she said, nudging them with her free foot. "You want more time, you pay for more time."

The Irsid grumbled and rose to their towering

height—nearly seven feet of spotted fur—and turned to leave the motel unceremoniously.

Alone in the room, Aster lay there for a moment to catch her breath, then sat up and dried her feet, realizing belatedly that her ankle was sore. Good thing that session *wasn't* extended. The vast majority of her clients never deliberately tried to hurt her; they were just much stronger and not used to the anatomy of fragile humans.

She limped on her throbbing ankle all the way back to her apartment, which meant she'd need a clinic visit—it had been just over a week since the last one.

Back at her place, she sank rapidly into a chair and propped her leg up. She was already looking forward to bathing, especially before spending several hours in the waiting room, hurting and tired, but at least clean.

Before the shower, she pulled up her finance account on her comm, which displayed an impressive number since she had just been paid. But with a few taps, a majority of the funds were transferred to a secure server where she would never see them again, and her own share was back to being dismal. In the process, she saw the remaining debt she still owed; the number always seemed absurd—like a joke. But after a year on Victory, she had made a dent, and all she had to do was power through this work long enough to get it paid off in full. Then she'd be free.

Dry and dressed with a brace in place on her ankle, Aster found that she was actually looking forward to seeing Dr.

Nova again—so that was a brand-new emotion about going to the clinic. She knew better than to start liking her too much, though, since no one that pleasant would possibly remain on Victory for long.

On her way, the station was beginning its daylight cycle, growing slightly brighter as she stopped to buy a breakfast sandwich. When she checked in at the front desk, the nurse scanned her wrist chip as usual, but then did a double take at Aster's profile.

"Oh," they said, brows raised. "Follow me right this way."

"Wh— what?" she asked, following the nurse.

Alone in an exam room moments later, Aster was still confused. She'd only taken two bites of the sandwich when Dr. Nova appeared with her signature warm smile and big, lively gray-blue eyes. Aster was still getting used to her demeanor—Dr. Nova must be close to her own age, but her positive energy made her seem younger, somehow. The opposite of Dr. Rylen in every possible way.

"Good morning, Aster! I hear it's your ankle today? Feel free to finish your breakfast while I take a look!"

Normally, a nurse would come in and take a preliminary scan when Aster finally got a bed, but apparently they were skipping that step this time. As the doctor scanned her ankle and Aster awkwardly chewed, it dawned on her that Dr. Nova might have given her some kind of special clearance after her last appointment. The thought was both touching and nerve-wracking. Dr. Nova had never lived on a station before, which meant she was from a planet, and like most grounders, probably a little naive about galactic society. She didn't understand that she was being *way* too nice to a *hooker*.

With pain meds in her system, Aster was too tired to think anymore. She drifted into sleep while the healing lamp went to work.

She woke up some time later, when Dr. Nova was removing the lamp and rescanning.

"Beautiful," Dr. Nova said, as usual. "Is there anything else I can do for you?"

Aster shook her head and shifted to sit upright. "That's all, thank you. But . . . listen."

Dr. Nova raised her eyebrows and waited, her expression curious and welcoming. She was really very pretty, Aster had to admit. Dr. Nova's soft blonde hair was cropped short, obscuring her forehead and falling over the tops of her ears in a cute way. Despite her strong shoulders and unusual height—*very* tall for a grounder—she was anything but intimidating.

Aster swallowed. "I know you're new here and you just started this job, but I'd hate to mess anything up for you. You . . . really don't want to be associated with me in any way, and that includes giving me urgent treatment. I have a terrible reputation here for the work I do, but it's my only option for now. You seem really nice. I'd hate for you to get fired because of me."

Dr. Nova listened with an expression Aster couldn't read. "I appreciate your honesty. To be completely honest with you in return, I am horrified by the way your previous doctor treated you. There is absolutely no justification for withholding pain meds or letting you suffer through long delays, and I'm sorry you had to experience that. As long as you're my patient, I will provide the *best* possible care I can manage. Given your high-risk occupation, I consider it perfectly appropriate for you to have a High Priority status in our system."

Aster wasn't sure how to respond. "Alright," she said with a slight chuckle, "but if this blows up in your face, I *did* try to warn you."

"That you did." Dr. Nova spared a glance to the side and went on in a hushed voice. "Just between us, if anyone ever *does* challenge me on the fact that I'm doing my job *correctly*, that won't turn out very well for them." She closed that sentence with a confident wink. Aster felt briefly like she had drifted into an alternate cartoon dimension.

As she left the clinic after such a short visit, it felt strange for Aster to think that she still had a full day ahead of her. She could do *anything*, she mused as she passed over a bridge on the way back to her apartment. She could go *anywhere*, she reasoned, as she took the elevator. A whole day of *freedom*, she reflected while removing her shoes. So many *possibilities*, she thought, as she crawled into bed, swaddled herself in blankets, and promptly passed out.

✸ ✸ ✸

Three months into life on Victory, Aster had become firmly established as Cori's most frequent patient, and Cori was determined to make her appointments as pleasant as possible through fun conversation.

"I keep meaning to ask you," Cori said while the healing lamp was repairing a knee sprain, "if you have a tattoo for *this* station."

Aster nodded, bending her arm and pointing to the plant shape below her elbow. "Yeah, it's this one."

"Is that an olive branch?"

Aster nodded again. "The agriculture level here is one of the only pleasant parts, so I figured... why not?"

"Oh, I haven't been to that level! I'll have to make a point to go see it."

"I've never been to a planet, myself," Aster added, "so I'm probably easily impressed."

Cori was inwardly happy at how much more open Aster had been lately. The healing lamp on her knee beeped, and Cori turned to remove it and re-scan.

"If you ask me, there's nothing short of extraordinary about humans building cities in space and setting aside room for growing fresh crops. So I'm sure I'll be impressed, as well. As for your knee, it's good as new! Anything else today?"

Aster shook her head. "Thank you."

"My pleasure."

"You know," Aster said as she sat up in the treatment bed, "you might like the novel *Gardens in Space* by Sidra Chamberlin, it's—"

"Oh, yes, I do like it!" Cori replied. "I love it, in fact."

"Really? You've read it?" Aster smiled in surprise.

Cori nodded. "It was one of my favorites while I was attending college. I especially like her optimistic vision for the future of species integration."

"Yeah, that story always stays with me."

"Now, have you read *Chronicles of Expansion* by Fiana Santrine?" Cori asked.

"I don't know that one."

"Hmm. Maybe worth a try. I have a hunch."

"I will," Aster said. "Thank you, again."

After she'd gone, Cori couldn't stop smiling about their chat all day. She was already looking forward to Aster's thoughts on the book. She decided to make it a point to visit the agriculture level soon, as well, both because it sounded fascinating and because it would give them more to discuss.

Maybe this could be the beginning of a real friendship.

On her free day later that week, Cori woke up excited for a new adventure to the agricultural level. The farming zones were open to the public, but for viewing only in the growing and harvest areas—and there was a market selling the freshest produce on the station, so the morning train was crowded with determined grocery shoppers on their way to the station's topmost level.

When she departed the train at the platform, the first thing Cori noticed was the scent of the air. It wasn't like the air on the lower levels—it smelled *green*, not unlike stepping outdoors on a planet. It was also much warmer here, so she took advantage of the rentable lockers and left her jacket behind.

Following a path toward the entrance of the growing section, the smell of plants only grew stronger. Cori found herself in a little oasis, with dozens of towers of leafy greens, and cultivators milling about on floating discs that could rise and fall to any level they needed. The equipment was worn, and the structures were patched up in many places, but the crops themselves were lush and well-kept. The people were clearly dedicated to their work.

It was abundantly clear why Aster enjoyed visiting this place—somewhat oddly, Cori found that the mere knowledge of Aster's fondness for it enriched the experience for her.

Wandering the visitor path through the growing field, she came across a cluster of children listening to an instructor and stopped to observe their lesson: they were identifying various plants and giving examples of food dishes that used them.

"A long time ago," the teacher explained, "these plants would have only grown in great big fields on Earth. But when our ancestors left that planet, they made sure to bring seeds along, so they could stay healthy in their new life in space. Now, we've perfected the technologies and methods needed to help these plants thrive without a natural sun. That means we can survive anywhere in the galaxy."

Cori marveled for a moment, as the lesson was in stark contrast to her own childhood education. She never consumed fresh plants back then—it was all protein packs and liquid meals. History lessons had been a side note to combat strategy. The desolate planet where she grew up bore no resemblance to the ancient Earth this teacher described.

She shook off the memories, moving on and passing around the class with a polite nod.

On her way home with a sack of fresh vegetables for stew, Cori was already looking forward to telling Aster all about her visit. Without really meaning to, she started daydreaming about how that conversation might go, imagining describing the smells and the students and the things she'd purchased, and then she caught herself and smiled. Did most people invent fake conversations with friends or acquaintances? She couldn't be sure since she was rarely so excited to see anyone. Or, in therapy speak, she "struggled to form lasting attachments." But there was no denying her fondness for this person.

Maybe she was already evolving in her new spacer life. She felt very lucky to have met Aster, for so many reasons.

✷ ✷ ✷

*What kind of gasbrain has a **crush** on their **doctor**?*

This kind of gasbrain, Aster asked and answered in her head as she downloaded yet another book from the station archive. Because if Dr. Nova recommended it, she was going to read it immediately so that they could talk about it at her next appointment. It had become a habit now for them to suggest things to each other—first the agriculture level a few weeks back, which Dr. Nova greatly enjoyed and spoke of at length. More recently, Aster had mentioned a couple of serials that Dr. Nova seemed excited to watch.

Aster's clinic appointments, once a source of ever-present dread, had become the highlight of her life on Victory. Because she was *clearly* a gasbrain.

She's a doctor! She's nice to me because I'm a patient! She's equally nice to everyone else!

Several points were made.

She also has a beautiful smile and great taste in fiction and might be the kindest person I've ever met.

Additional, and undeniably true, points.

Why am I like this?

The mystery went unsolved.

Then again, maybe it made sense that Aster had "imprinted" on Dr. Nova in this way; it wasn't like she had any other friends on this station. Life on Victory would hardly be manageable *without* devouring books and serials and films in her free time, and it had been a long time since she had anyone to discuss them with.

So that was all fine, but why did she feel giddy every time she thought of Dr. Nova?

Fucking gasbrain.

After losing several hours of the day to the engrossing book, Aster decided to go out and grab some dinner—and hopefully occupy her mind with something other than a thoroughly hopeless crush.

The second wish did not come true.

On her way back to her apartment with her meal, she spotted a familiar blonde head across the road and stopped in her tracks.

Dr. Nova must live nearby, Aster realized. As much as she would have liked to talk to her, she took a few steps back to avoid being noticed. Dr. Nova was dressed casually and having a conversation with the owner of a repair shop. From afar, Aster got the sense that they knew each other—he was probably another patient.

See? She's nice to everyone, Aster reminded herself.

Just then, there was a loud crash, and Aster's gaze snapped over to where a hauler had backed into the base of a thick metal post—one that held the only remaining sliver of an old archway over the road. The anchor must have been rusted through because the impact was enough to topple it, falling in slow motion as people scrambled to get out of its path.

Aster looked quickly back at Dr. Nova, only to find her moving *toward* the post. Was she completely insane?

"Stop!" Aster said, starting forward, her voice lost in the crowd.

And then, as if it were the most natural thing to do, Dr. Nova caught the post. Aster watched in growing disbelief as Dr. Nova held it steady and eased it down so that it settled to the ground with a tap—instead of a brain-rattling bang.

Looking around to see if anyone else was as bewildered as she was, Aster only saw people going back to their original business, milling about as if nothing out of the ordinary had happened. Maybe the post wasn't as heavy as she thought, after wearing down with age. How else could a single person hold it?

It took Aster a moment to spot Dr. Nova again; she had crouched down to speak to a child, taking a look at the scrapes on their face and arm, and then sending them off with a pat on the shoulder.

Aster continued home, still confused—and more than a little unsettled—by what she had seen. There were body mods that could hypothetically make someone that strong, but they had long been illegal across the galaxy.

WHERE STARLIGHT BURNS

In the end, she was just glad Dr. Nova hadn't been hurt. Even if she, apparently, had some secrets.

✸ ✸ ✸

Back in a treatment bed the following week, Aster found that the incident on the street faded from her mind as soon as she saw Dr. Nova's warm smile.

"I'm so glad you told me about *Asterism Entangled*," Dr. Nova said as she set up a healing lamp on Aster's shoulder. "I'm honestly kind of addicted—I've been watching it every night."

Aster kept her cool, reminding herself that *lots* of people loved that serial and this shared interest didn't *mean* anything. "I'm glad you like it! It keeps getting better, in my opinion."

"That's good to hear!" Dr. Nova said. "Well, I do wish I could stay and talk to you for the whole session today, but unfortunately, there are others waiting."

"Oh, of course, I understand! I'm fine here."

"Good. I'll be back shortly."

With that, Aster was alone in the room. It was clearly absurd to think that the friendly Dr. Nova could be hiding anything serious about her past—or her abilities. But Aster also knew very little about the doctor's life before she ended up on Victory.

The thought prompted a pang of desire. She wished she

could know more about Dr. Nova, wished she knew her well enough to ask about that stunt with the post. She wished they could grow closer and watch serials together and meet up outside of the damned clinic. But all of that was pure fantasy, for so many reasons.

The lamp beeped and shut off a short time later, then Dr. Nova reappeared. Aster felt a pathetic prickle at the corners of her eyes at the thought of their brief time together already ending. She didn't want to go back to her lonely apartment and wait days or weeks to be hurt again just so she could see her only "friend."

"Beautiful," Dr. Nova said upon rescanning. "Are you alright?"

"Yes," Aster replied, snapping back to reality. "I'm great, now. Thank you."

"My pleasure. See you next time—but hopefully not *too* soon. Be careful out there."

"Of course," Aster said. "Not too soon. See you then."

3

Parasite

Perhaps one of the only benefits of the cold, chaotic world where Cori grew up was that it had made her well prepared for disaster. There was hardly a medical crisis that could compare to the endless warfare she witnessed in her youth. As a soldier, she had been conditioned to focus on a single task under any circumstances.

So, five months into her position at clinic 4H, when the ER was suddenly overflowing with burn victims after an explosion on the engineering level, she leapt into action without hesitation. First, she requested that the night shift doctor be called in to assist. Second, she attended to the patients with the most severe injuries, instructing nurses to alert her to any whose conditions became critical.

The patients in her clinic were in better shape than those transferred to larger hospitals, so, working in tandem with the second physician, they were able to care for all patients within about five hours. She found true beauty in the way they were all working so hard to help and to heal as efficiently as possible; she was glad to be a part of it.

Late into the night, at a time when her own shift would normally have ended, Cori was between patients when a nurse named Thiago stopped her, looking frazzled. "Dr. Nova, a high-priority patient arrived in critical condition a few minutes ago. There's no room here, so she's upstairs."

That information created an odd crack in Cori's calm. She had only personally given one patient that status.

"What symptoms? And the patient's name?"

"It's Aster Moss. She came in with severe abdominal pain and bleeding from—"

"Shit!" The exclamation slipped out before she could stop herself. "Has anyone scanned her?"

"They were in the process of scanning when I came—"

"Good. I'll be in there as soon as I can."

"Yes, doctor," Thiago agreed, hurrying away.

Quickly taking stock of the ER floor, Cori confirmed that all patients were stable and put her assistant physician in charge. Then she hurried up to the next floor to find her friend.

She knew she'd found the right hallway when she heard Aster cry out. Which meant that she was alive and awake, at least.

Cori entered the treatment room to find Aster doubled over, clutching her stomach and coughing up bright red blood. When Cori stepped up beside her, she could see that blood had soaked into the white sheets below Aster's seat, too, and her heart sank. This looked far worse than her previous injuries.

"Aster, it's Dr. Nova," she said, gently touching her shoulder. "I'm here to help you."

Instead of responding with words, Aster flopped back into the bed, writhing and crying out again, clutching her stomach.

"Give her four doses of AnoDyn, and where's that scan?"

Thiago handed over the tablet with a look of silent horror. When Cori checked the screen, she could see why: There was a live organism in Aster's gut—one Cori didn't recognize. It was alien. And it was eating her alive.

There was only one possible course of action.

"Prep for surgical extraction immediately."

"Dr. Nova, the surgical suite here isn't used for extensive—"

Cori exhaled an impatient breath. "There's no time to discuss options. Prep her now."

Thanks to the pain meds, Aster had calmed, but she was crying steadily into her pillow—and still coughing a tired little cough as more blood came up.

"Aster," Cori said, "we're going to put you under now, and I'll get that thing out of you."

Aster looked at her with sheer terror in her eyes.

"I don't want to die," she sobbed through bloody teeth.

Cori touched her shoulder again, holding her gaze. "You are *not* going to die today. I promise."

Seconds later, Aster was unconscious, and they transferred her into the clinic's small surgical suite. By the time Cori was ready to operate, a bio-analyst had arrived with a portable cryo-chamber for collection of the parasite, so at least *someone* else was thinking fast (and Cori's flimsy plan to drop it on the floor and crush it under her boot wouldn't have to be put into action).

The creature was large enough to be easy to locate; it didn't put up much of a fight when she seized it with her tongs and wrenched it out of the abdominal cavity. Wriggling there at the end of the metal tool, it was long and blue and shimmery in the light, though covered in blood and possibly dying. It never expected to be in a human host, of course. After it was deposited into the carrier, promptly frozen, and whisked away by the eager analyst, Cori turned her attention back to Aster—time for the real work to begin.

Over the next several hours, she located and repaired the damage to the internal organs. Given that it was spread out in an unpredictable pattern, she checked each centimeter of tissue for damage with unwavering precision, using small, handheld healing wands over any injuries. Some areas appeared to have been forcibly attacked, while others were marred with odd splotches that looked like chemical burns. Each one called for a healing wand of a certain size and a unique calibration. As she worked, she was increasingly confident that she could fix everything, as long as Aster could hold on long enough. Nearly the whole digestive tract was in tatters—the parasite had taken a full tour, then punched a hole in the intestinal wall to explore the abdomen. When she reached the end of the interior damage, she moved to examine the patient's mouth and pelvic area, confirming no external damage under the patches of dried blood. It was unclear how the creature entered, but it could have been much smaller when Aster acquired it, Cori reflected.

It was only after closing her up and healing the incision that Cori learned the surgery had taken eleven hours in total—the nurses looked ready to pass out after such a long shift, so she praised their good work and sent them home to rest for the next day. While Aster was being transported back to her treatment room, Cori returned to the ER floor and was glad to hear that all burn patients had been dismissed.

As she was starting back toward Aster's room, a nurse stopped her—Thiago, the same nurse who took the scan of the parasite, now out of uniform. "Dr. Nova, do you have a moment?"

"Yes."

"That surgery was . . . amazing. That was amazing to watch. I didn't think she had a chance."

There was regret and confession in his tone, as much as there was awe. Cori heard what he *wasn't* saying.

"You helped save a life today, and you learned," she told him. "That's a success."

"Thank you," he said, likely too exhausted to find other words.

Back in Aster's room, Cori pulled up a chair to sit beside her. Aster was still unconscious, but her brow furrowed and relaxed a few times, suggesting that she would wake up shortly. Cori could feel the full weight of her own fatigue now that her body was relaxed, but she couldn't even think of leaving. She wouldn't let Aster wake up alone after what she had endured.

When Aster's eyes started to open, Cori took her hand to help ground her. It was a friendly gesture more than a doctoral one, but it felt right. "There you are."

Aster's hazy gaze found her, and she stared blankly for a moment.

"How are you feeling?"

Aster hummed in reply. "Tired." Realization passed over her face. "What—what happened? What was that thing?"

Cori could see on the monitors that Aster's heart rate had spiked, so she took Aster's hand into a firm grasp between her own. "Listen, you're going to be fine. It was some kind of alien parasite, but I was able to repair all the damage. When the analyst sends back results, I can tell you what it—"

"No," Aster said, closing her eyes and shaking her head. "I don't want to know."

"Okay."

With her eyes still closed, she took a deep breath and licked her dry lips.

"Would you like a drink of water?"

Aster nodded at that, and Cori stood to grab a cup with a straw. After drinking, Aster was clearly on the brink of sleep again, so Cori told her to rest and checked her scans one last time to be sure everything still looked perfect.

"I finished the book," Aster mumbled, eyes still closed.

It took a moment for Cori to recall the last one she had recommended. "Oh, you did? And?"

A slow smile spread across Aster's face. "You were right. It was amazing."

An odd feeling passed over Cori at that moment. A powerful and passionate fondness, like nothing she had ever felt before. In an instant, she realized the extent of her relief that Aster was still here with her. Any other outcome would have been an unfathomable loss. So unimaginable, in fact, that she had been emotionally blind to that possibility while she worked to save her.

"Good," Cori managed, swallowing a lump. "I'm so glad you did."

✳ ✳ ✳

The next afternoon, after being discharged and sleeping nearly a full day in her apartment, Aster was on her way back to the clinic. It felt a little strange, to be headed there in the light of day—and without any injuries.

She was carrying a box of exotic fruit she picked up

at the central markets and had wrapped, as a gift, for Dr. Nova. It wasn't lost on her that her incident with the space bug came at the worst possible time, what with something *exploding* somewhere and the clinic being at capacity. In the midst of all that, Dr. Nova had gone above and beyond to save her life. Aster needed to acknowledge that in some way, even if the best she could do was fruit.

At the clinic, she found the front desk empty, which meant the nurse was preoccupied. After waiting a while with no one appearing, Aster realized this could be a good thing. She decided to try her luck visiting Dr. Nova's office, since she knew her way around the clinic pretty well.

Down the hall and around two corners, she came upon the Head Physician office and found the door partly ajar, and then realized she could hear voices inside—one of them was Dr. Nova, but she didn't recognize the other.

Then she realized what the unfamiliar voice was saying.

"What I need you to explain to me is why you abandoned the emergency floor during a crisis so that you could...ugh, so that you could perform an *unapproved* surgical extraction on a *hooker*."

Aster's heart was abruptly in her throat. She knew she shouldn't be listening, but she was frozen in place.

"I'm disturbed by your choice of words, director, but I'm more than happy to explain," came Dr. Nova's admirably calm response. "I did not abandon the floor. After learning that I had a patient in critical condition upstairs,

I confirmed that all ER patients were stable and put Dr. Turnor in charge. And then, as you know, I performed urgent, life-saving surgery on the patient."

"That's not an acceptable answer! Patients in need of extensive surgery are to be transferred to 3H—you know that. And the patients coming in from the *accident* should have been your first priority. Someone who chooses to engage in *unsafe* behavior is not."

Aster hated everything about this moment, especially because she knew it would happen. She *knew* Dr. Nova's kindness to her would backfire eventually. Readjusting the package in her arms and trying not to breathe too loudly, she realized her hands were shaking.

There was a pause before Dr. Nova responded. When she did, Aster was stunned by the tone of her voice.

"Excuse me, director, but you hired me to run this clinic, and I intend to decide according to my best judgment at any moment which patients need my personal attention. I had a floor full of stable burn victims with mild to moderate injuries, and one patient upstairs in critical condition with no time to spare. I made the only ethical choice, and I would do it again a thousand times. Further—please let me finish. Further, the patient in question is one of the *many* human residents on this station that *you* have personally vowed to keep safe, and I have vowed to keep alive. If you have any sincere issues with my performance, you can take them to the advisory board, but I cannot and will not accept that I should have simply let my patient *die*."

Immediately after Dr. Nova stopped speaking, Aster could hear footsteps and made the quick decision to stand on the opposite side of the doorway, watching as the director went stomping in the other direction. He vanished so quickly, Aster couldn't be sure if he noticed her standing there.

Alone in the hall again, Aster looked down at the gift and sighed. It could not possibly be the right time, she reasoned, and moved sadly away.

Just as she reached the corner, there came a voice behind her.

"Aster?"

She turned to find Dr. Nova approaching, warm and friendly as always, despite the highly unpleasant conversation she had experienced.

"Nice to see you looking well," Dr. Nova said. Her expression shifted. "Are you in to see me?"

Something about standing in a hall and facing her at eye level was the tiniest bit surreal; Dr. Nova was just a couple inches taller than her, she realized. And Aster wasn't sure if it was the lighting, but Dr. Nova somehow looked even more attractive than usual, a hint of color in her cheeks.

"No. Well, yes. I mean . . . I don't have an *appointment*. I just wanted to bring this to you."

"Oh, how thoughtful. Want to step inside my office?"

Inside, Dr. Nova shut the door, and Aster glanced around the little room. There was a plain desk and chairs, plus a small shelf...full of other gifts. But of course everyone loved Dr. Nova. Of course.

"How are you feeling today?" Dr. Nova asked, unwrapping the box.

"Oh, I feel fine, thanks to you. I wanted to...I wanted to be sure you know how grateful I am."

"Oh, yum!" Dr. Nova said upon seeing the fruit. "These look delicious. I can't wait to try them. But I hope you know they weren't necessary. Seeing you fully recovered is all the thanks I need."

"I know it was the worst possible time," Aster said, her voice wavering. "And I know...I know I would have died without you. I know that."

She awkwardly wiped her eyes, and in the fleeting blindness that followed, she didn't see Dr. Nova step around the desk until she was already pulling her into an embrace. Aster readily returned the hug, wrapping her arms tightly around her, unable to fight the sobs that escaped.

"Hey, it's okay," Dr. Nova was saying. "It wasn't your fault. I'm so glad you're alright."

"I'm sorry," Aster blurted. "I'm sorry I caused trouble for you."

"What?" Dr. Nova asked, leaning back to look her in the eyes. "What do you— Oh, no. Were you listening when the director—?"

Aster nodded, sheepishly.

Dr. Nova sighed, shaking her head. "Aster, you haven't caused me any trouble, and you don't owe me any apologies. I'm sorry you heard any part of that. Don't waste two seconds of thought on him, alright? I consider you a friend, and my time on this station has only been improved by knowing you."

Aster smiled, feeling some of her tension evaporate. Dr. Nova pulled her into a second hug, which she eagerly returned.

"I consider you a friend, too," Aster said when they were facing each other again. "I really enjoy all our conversations."

"Likewise. I wish I could stay and talk to you all afternoon, but unfortunately, I have to get back to work."

"Of course."

Dr. Nova gave her a look. "You know, I really *would* like to keep talking to you outside of this clinic. I hope this isn't too forward, but would you like to meet for dinner sometime?"

It took Aster several seconds to form a response. It was like her brain broke and she forgot how to answer a question.

"Maybe another ti—" Dr. Nova started.

"It's not that I don't *want* to," Aster rushed to explain. "I just can't. It's too risky. If the wrong people saw us out together... that could be bad for you. Worse than defending me in a medical sense."

"I'm not sure I understand, but I wouldn't want you to

be uncomfortable. You'd be welcome to join me for dinner in my apartment, if that would be better?"

"Oh," Aster said, wholly unprepared for the offer. "Uh, yes? Sure! I'd like that."

"Wonderful!" Dr. Nova's whole face lit up. "How's tomorrow night, then?"

"Great," Aster said with an awkward laugh. "I mean, *I* don't have any plans."

Dr. Nova smiled. They shared contact information across their comms. Aster hoped it wasn't too obvious that her hands were shaking again.

"See you tomorrow," Dr. Nova said as they stepped back into the hall.

"Thanks, Dr. Nova."

"I think you can call me Cori, now," she said softly, patting Aster's shoulder and then continuing on her way.

Once again, Aster's brain needed a moment to reboot.

4

The Truth

Cori had anticipated that her new life in space would bring surprises and new experiences, but somehow, *inviting a friend over for dinner* was the most exciting development so far. Yes, heading her own clinic was going well, and the station itself had started to feel like home, but those were things she expected. Meeting someone whose company she enjoyed as much as Aster was truly incredible.

As she prepared a pot of soup for them to share, she couldn't recall the last time she had been so happy about a simple meal. Every time she pictured Aster seated at her table, Cori's heart did an odd little flutter. She wasn't sure what to make of that, but she reasoned that it must be because this was the first time they were meeting outside of the clinic.

But when Aster finally arrived at her door looking more stunning than Cori had ever seen, all *reasonable* explanations for her excitement vanished. Instead of her normal casual look, Aster had lined her eyes with dark makeup, donned a shimmery purple top under a black jacket, and swept her fiery hair to one side in a thick braid.

"Welcome!" Cori managed when she remembered how to speak. "Please come in!"

Aster smiled, giving her an odd look as she entered. Cori belatedly realized her enthusiasm might have been a little heavy.

"There's soup for dinner," she said, in a more even tone. "I hope that's alright."

"That sounds perfect," Aster said, giving the place a once-over. There wasn't much to see in the living room—just a basic sofa, wall screen, window, and the corner shelves, which caught Aster's eye. "Oh, wow, are those *paper* books?"

"Yes!" Cori confirmed, delighted to have something to talk about. "I collect them. Not easy to find, and fragile, but they're so fascinating. Feel free to take a closer look."

Aster stepped over to the shelf and tilted her head to read a few spines, which Cori found deeply endearing. She offered her a pair of reading gloves, and Aster turned a few pages of *The Greek Myths*, elegantly clothbound and gold embossed.

"Isn't it neat?" Cori said. "Holding them feels like traveling back in time, to me."

Aster nodded. "I feel that, too."

As she set the book on the shelf and carefully picked up

another, Cori watched eagerly, noticing how gently Aster opened the cover and ran her gloved fingers over a page, the fabric sliding across the paper with a light brushing sound. Suddenly, Cori realized her heart was pounding, and she had to snap herself out of intense-focus mode. She had always enjoyed Aster's company, but that enjoyment felt different here, somehow, with the way she was standing there looking *so* beautiful and admiring Cori's little collection and—

"Thank you," Aster said abruptly, handing back the gloves. "I appreciate you showing me."

"Of course!" Cori said. The enthusiasm was definitely too strong again. "I'm ... happy to know you share my appreciation for them."

"Very much ... Uh, the soup smells delicious?"

"Oh, yes! Dinner!"

Seated at the table moments later, Cori took a moment to calm herself. Never in her life had she felt so endeared to another person. Anytime she looked at Aster, there came an odd rush of heat to her face. Cori knew the human body inside and out, and she inwardly chastised herself for letting this feeling perplex her. It was obvious what was happening, of course: She didn't *only* desire friendship with Aster. There was physical and emotional attraction present, as well. A "crush," it would commonly be called, only ... she'd never had one before.

She met her eyes and smiled, and Aster smiled back. Yes, this was a *crush*. There could be no other possible word for it. It was the same feeling she had when Aster recovered from the surgery, and when she brought the gift to her office.

"Oh, are these—?" Aster asked, noticing the sliced fruits Cori had set out.

"Yes! I thought we could try a few of them together," Cori said, sipping her drink.

Aster smiled again and took a slice, closing her eyes as she savored a bite.

So *this* was a crush, Cori mused. Assigning a name to the feeling put her more at ease, and they fell into easy conversation like always. Cori spoke of her time on Idun working on her medical training, and Aster shared memories of Centauride Station, where she grew up as the only child of three mothers and attended school.

It was a gift, Cori reflected, to know Aster at all. To be able to spend such a wonderful evening with her was the sort of exceptionally beautiful experience that the universe so rarely offered, a gem within the stardust.

"This is nice," Aster said after they had finished their bowls. "Having a conversation while I'm not under one of your healing lamps."

"It's a very nice change, yes." Cori nodded. "Although, I have to admit that I've started looking forward to your appointments—not the reasons for them, of course, but the chance to see you. Is that strange to say?"

Aster shook her head. "Not at all. I've been looking forward to them, too. I'm glad you invited me here."

"I couldn't agree more."

Cori regarded her for some time, making sure to capture this moment in her mind.

"Cori," Aster said with a curious smile, "are you feeling okay?"

Cori laughed, realizing how obviously she was staring. Hearing Aster use her first name was strangely moving. She made a decision, then, knowing it might be the wrong one. But she had long known not to take anything beautiful for granted.

"I'm much better than okay. In fact... I want to tell you something."

"Oh?"

"I learned a long time ago not to leave anything important unsaid. So, I just want you to know how glad I am that we're friends—"

"I'm glad, too," Aster said, looking slightly confused.

"But the truth for me," Cori went on, "is that I also have romantic feelings for you. And I want you to know that, because I don't know if there will ever be a better time to tell you."

Wide-eyed, Aster's gaze shifted down to her lap. "I'm sorry."

"Oh, no, you have nothing to apologize for!" Cori said, scrambling to better explain herself. "I wasn't assuming anything; I just wanted to be completely honest with you. I'm sorry if that was too forward."

"No," Aster said, in contrast to her expression. "Not too forward, just . . . I can't . . . I wasn't expecting . . . I'm *very* touched, Cori. You're one of the kindest, most interesting people I've ever met, and I'm really glad to be your...friend. This is the best night I've had in ages."

Cori appreciated the words, but she could tell Aster was uncomfortable. It figured that Cori would fumble this interaction in some way. She moved to collect the dishes and remarked about how glad she was that the soup turned out alright. Aster seemed relieved by the shift back to light conversation, eagerly agreeing and calling it "so delicious" several times.

Later that night, Cori reflected happily on the evening they passed together. Even with Aster's baffled reaction to her sudden confession, Cori was glad she had been honest—if something terrible happened and she never saw Aster again, she could harbor no regrets.

As she laid in bed, she found herself thinking about all the poems and songs about love, spanning back centuries of human history. With so much emphasis on the *agony* of unrequited crushes, Cori had always imagined that it must be a miserable and maddening experience, the sort of thing that she'd be wise to avoid. But in reality, the complete opposite was true. Her feelings for Aster were wholly pleasant, and she was grateful to be experiencing them.

✳ ✳ ✳

As it turned out, a few days of reflection was all it took for Cori's serenity to become warped with doubt, her previous satisfaction with her honesty having faded.

For one thing, Aster would probably have no interest in sharing future meals together. For another, and much greater concern, Aster might feel less comfortable about coming back to the clinic for treatment.

That thought had Cori's stomach in knots, because it was the opposite of what she wanted for *any* patient. Logic told her that Aster wouldn't be swayed when she needed healing, but in hindsight, Cori hated to think that she might have done something that would crack the solid foundation of trust they had built over several months.

Was she really so caught up in a beautiful moment that she failed to think of Aster's future as a patient? Maybe crushes were messy, maddening things after all.

Cori was composing an apology message in her head for the tenth time when she stepped into her office and did a double take to find Dr. Davis once again waiting for her. Something about his demeanor seemed off. Reluctant, perhaps.

"Hello, Dr. Nova," he said with forced politeness, uncharacteristically avoiding eye contact.

"Director, is there something I can help you with?"

"Yes, actually," he said with a sigh. "We need to have a conversation."

Alicia Haberski

✷ ✷ ✷

In the days that followed the surreal evening with Cori, Aster felt a bit like her head was spinning. On the one hand, she had a wonderful time with her only friend on the station.

On the other hand, what the *fuck* just happened?

The idea of someone like Cori expressing interest in her would be almost *hilarious* if it weren't so dangerous. Part of her had wanted to yell, "Did you hear *anything* I've told you about my reputation?" But thankfully, that part had been suppressed under her much kinder response.

It pained her to think that she had technically rejected Cori by letting her assume that she didn't reciprocate her feelings. If Aster's situation were different, she wouldn't have hesitated to be honest . . . and maybe even spend the night with her. But things weren't so simple. It was better this way, Aster reasoned, to keep it an amicable friendship, to keep Cori at arm's length. No matter how much guilt pooled in her mind like dark bile, clouding over any thoughts of her friend.

She had no idea if things would be different between them when they saw each other next.

That would be soon, she realized, when she woke up with a throbbing elbow. She hadn't worked again yet—she'd decided to take a break after the insanity with the parasite— but her elbow had been cranky lately. After taking some basic painkillers, the discomfort felt like it might fade as usual, but as she moved around, it only tripled, radiating pain through her arm. She was promptly on her way to the clinic.

Aster was so distracted by thinking about seeing Cori again that she missed what the nurse was saying at the front desk.

"Sorry, what?"

"You've been reassigned. You need to report to clinic 3H."

"Reassigned?" she repeated, as if they weren't speaking the same language.

"That's right. This isn't your clinic anymore."

Aster felt frozen. A few people had queued behind her.

"But I normally see Dr. Nova—"

"She isn't *here* anymore," the nurse said, impatient. "Do you need me to order a medical transport to 3H?"

"No, no thanks... I can get there on my own."

As she turned to leave, Aster felt like there was a weight on her chest, making it hard to breathe or think. For a moment, she had no idea what to do. She wanted to just go home, but one tiny movement reminded her that her elbow was on fire.

On her way to the train platform, she was in such a weird haze that she even bumped into someone, thankfully not on the side of the bad elbow.

How could Cori be gone without saying anything? Did she get fired by that asshole director? Was she forced to leave

Victory? Did she *already* know when they had dinner together, and that's why she confessed her feelings?

The last thought hit Aster like a slap in the face. Maybe Cori *did* know that she was going to have to leave—she had said all that stuff about wanting to tell Aster the truth while she had the chance. And then Aster had just sat there. What if she never saw her again?

Clinic 3H was in a bigger hospital in the station's central hub, an area that Aster hadn't spent much time in after being snubbed at a salon about a year ago—she'd started trimming her own hair and sticking to her own zone after that. That made her less than optimistic about how the staff at *this* clinic would treat her.

The train platform here was bigger and busier than in her zone; she exited in a crowd of other humans. This area might have been nice once, back when the hotels were fancy enough to attract actual tourists, half the shops weren't closed, and the statues were recognizable shapes rather than crumbling blobs.

The new clinic turned out to be much larger than the one Aster was used to, and the lobby was confusing since there wasn't just one simple reception desk, but she finally made her way to someone who could scan her ID.

"Ah, Aster Moss. Yes, you're in the right place. What's the appointment for?"

"Just elbow pain. Tendonitis, I think."

"Alright, that's all set. Follow me."

For a moment, she wondered if maybe the special clearance Cori gave her was still in the system, but then she realized that *this* clinic probably had plenty of openings. Figures that she got stuck with the shitty one all this time.

Seated in a treatment room moments later, she waited. A nurse came in and took a scan of her elbow. Aster barely noticed what he said. She was eager to get this over with so she could go home and sleep, even though she doubted she'd be able to sleep at all. After the nurse left, she realized she had no idea how long she'd be left waiting at this new clinic.

Then the door opened.

"Aster!" Cori said, stepping inside, bright and chipper as ever. "So sorry for the shuffling. I just found out yesterday they were moving me here, and I put you on my transfer list, but I hadn't had the chance to tell you, and— Oh. Are you alright?"

Aster had started to laugh when Cori came in as the pieces clicked into place and she realized how silly it had been to be worried. But the laugh had quickly dissolved into ugly tears.

"I thought you were—ugh," Aster said, awkwardly wiping her eyes. "I didn't know where you—"

"Oh, no," Cori said, coming closer. "I thought they would have explained ... Oh, I'm so sorry. I never thought for a second that you might think I left without saying something. I wouldn't do that."

Aster moved to hug her with her good arm. Cori very gently returned the embrace.

"I'm sorry," she said again. "I should have made sure you knew what was going on."

At that, Aster pulled back to look at her again, bringing their faces closer than they had ever been. Cori was looking at her with such heartfelt concern that for the briefest moment, Aster *almost* gave in and kissed her. Instead, she sat up straight.

"It's okay—I'm fine," Aster said. "I'm really glad you had me transferred over with you."

"Of course I did!" Cori said, then her smile fell a bit. "Actually, I'm very glad to hear you say that. I owe you another apology, though. I shouldn't have been so candid at dinner, and I hope I didn't put you in an awkward position as my patient. I hope you know that your treatment here will always be my first—"

"No, Cori," Aster interrupted, shaking her head. "It's okay. You don't need to apologize."

"I really think I do. I should have known better than to mention that. It wasn't appropriate. I'm very sorry."

Aster sighed. *Thank you,* she knew she should say. *Let's forget all about it and stay friends.*

"No . . . *I'm* sorry," she said instead. "I wasn't equally honest with you. The truth is . . . I do feel the same way about you. I have for a while. It's very mutual."

In the heavy silence that followed, Cori's expression

shifted to one Aster had never seen before—she looked genuinely stunned, and a bright blush had risen to her nose and cheeks.

"Oh," she said, swallowing. "Oh, but... you apologized to me? After I told you?"

Aster smiled at that, glancing down at the floor. "I was thinking that you fell for the worst possible person on the station... That's just what came out."

"Aw," Cori said in a lightly scolding tone. "That's not true."

"It's just that, with the kind of work I'm doing—"

Cori cut her off. "Oh, shit, your *elbow*! Let's get you scanned!"

Aster held her arm out, wincing, and Cori took a scan like usual. Her face was still rosy.

"Yes, there's some inflammation in the tendon here. That's, um. Well, it's a quick heal. But, gosh, I'm blanking on the term for it."

"Tendonitis?" Aster asked.

"Yes! That's it. Thank you! Alright. Let's get you under a lamp!"

As she reclined in the bed, Aster felt a little bad for springing the truth on Cori here, since it seemed like maybe she had scrambled her brain a little. Cori didn't even remember to give her pain meds until *after* the lamp was in place, and she wasn't as talkative as usual.

"Is everything alright?" Aster finally asked.

Cori's whole face bloomed scarlet. "Yes, I'm fine! I just . . . Well! I wish we had more time to, uh, to talk about... Would you want to come by later, maybe? My new place is here—up a few levels, I mean."

"Sure," Aster said. "I'll come by."

"Great," Cori said happily.

The lamp sounded its completion and Cori removed it, then rescanned Aster's elbow and confirmed it was fully healed.

When Aster stood from the bed, bringing them face to face, Cori gave her an awkward smile. "Sorry, again, about the surprise transfer. I'll see you later?"

Aster nodded in reply. They parted ways on a positive note, but she was already dreading the conversation to come and how disappointing it would be for both of them. By the time she was back on a train, the whole interaction was like a weird dream.

5

Scars

One and a half years ago

"Fuck! My tether just snapped!" Aster shouted inside her helmet, using the magnetic grip on her suit to hang onto the ship with one hand while finishing the repair with the other. A small impact had made a wonky panel pop right off the hull, so she was checking the insulation over some wiring and attaching a temporary cover. Not her best work, but also not her ship.

"Are you drifting?" came the reply, a little casual and a little late.

"No, I'm good. But someone's gonna have to grab me."

She didn't know these people well; she'd only taken this job a few days prior. They were smugglers who'd landed a big contract; if they could pull it off, her cut would be enough to set her up for a couple *years* without needing another job. That was too good to pass up.

Even if it meant tolerating this rustbucket ship and shitty suit.

Finishing the repair, she sealed the hole and began making her way back to the hatch. Given the lack of a cable, she crawled along the ship, made more difficult by the fact that her knee magnets were faulty and she had to rely on her hands. Most of the time, Aster enjoyed being in the void, but at this particular moment, she was very much ready to be back in the ship and get this damned job over with.

"Um, guys? Anyone else seeing this?" came the pilot's voice.

His tone wasn't helping Aster's nerves. At that moment, the magnet on her left hand stopped grabbing, suddenly, and then the right. She realized she'd hit a portion of the hull that had been patched up with a different type of metal. *Fucking rustbucket.*

"Hey, I need some help out here," she started, only to be interrupted by chaos on the comms.

With several people yelling at once, she couldn't figure out what they were reacting to, but it dawned on her to look behind her—at two explosions in the distance. Another shortly followed. The abandoned ships they'd come to collect had been blown to bits.

In her state of shock, she slipped off the side of the ship and failed to regain her hold.

"Oh, fuck, drifting! I'm drifting!"

"Hang tight, we got you, and then we're outta here. Some stealth ship just nuked those—wait, shit. What the fuck is that? What the fuck?"

"What's going on?!" Aster called, her distance from the ship steadily increasing.

"They're locked on—they won't respond—we're being—"

That was the final transmission before the flash: The little ship she'd been tethered to minutes ago exploded in a bright burst that reduced it to fragments.

For several minutes, Aster couldn't process it. Couldn't think in the quiet that followed. And then she did two things: She checked the oxygen supply on her suit and found twelve hours left, so that was a tiny source of comfort. Next, she made sure her emergency beacon was off. She didn't need to flag down the people who just *murdered her crew* to come finish the job. She'd have to turn it on eventually, but for now she'd wait. And drift.

"Well. Shit."

✱ ✱ ✱

Present

Never in Cori's entire medical career had she been so eager to leave work and go home. Even after her shift ended, she got caught in conversation with some new coworkers who had lots of questions. Apparently they'd decided to promote an assistant, but then that doctor had been shifted to 4H specifically so they could transfer Cori over here—word had spread about the unprecedented parasite removal surgery, and so 3H wanted her on their team.

She was happy to be there, and her new coworkers were lovely, but she *really* wanted to go back to her apartment.

When she was finally in the elevator on her way up, she sent a quick message to Aster and took a deep breath to calm herself.

The new apartment was bigger than the last one, with an extra room she hadn't found any use for, and a nice large window offering a partial view of the central hub. As she changed into a casual top and zipped up a cozy sweater, she took a moment to ground herself, taking more calming breaths and thinking of what she would say to Aster. Cori had been thoroughly caught off guard at the clinic, but this time, she would be prepared and composed.

Aster arrived shortly, and Cori managed to greet her in an even, polite way before they took to the sofa, where Cori had set out two glasses of water, unsure what else to do.

"I'm glad you could come. I thought we could have a real conversation and figure out if we both want the same things."

Aster nodded but said nothing.

"Personally," Cori went on. "I'm interested in a romantic relationship, if that's also what you want."

Aster looked at her with sad eyes. "I meant what I said earlier. I feel the same way you do. But with my reputation . . . it's risky for you to be seen with someone like me. Genuinely. That asshole director guy isn't the only one who thinks like that. I don't want to cost you your job."

Cori considered that. "I appreciate you looking out for me, but I'm going to ask you to please not worry about that. He's an asshole, yes, but he's not going to fire me. And, frankly, anyone who shares his views about your occupation is not someone whose opinion matters to me."

"You're not the head of a clinic anymore, though," Aster observed. "Is that not . . . a demotion?"

"Oh gosh, no—nearly the opposite. They requested me here since this clinic is equipped for more complex procedures."

"Oh," Aster said. "That's good, then."

"I know that I'm still new to all this, and I can't possibly understand what you've been through here, but . . . public reputation is not something that will ever concern me. Is that all that worries you?"

"No," Aster said. "Another is that if we dated . . . it probably wouldn't end well. And I really can't handle *you* hating me. I can handle it from everyone else, but not you. Whatever rosy future you're picturing, it's not possible."

Cori's heart was pounding, but she managed to reply calmly. "What do you think might happen between us?"

Aster sighed, shifting to better face her. "You know

exactly how dangerous my work is. You've seen me on my worst day ever. How long before you ask me to stop? Before you tell me it's not worth it? Because, look, I'd probably say those same things to me if I were someone else. But I need the money, and I need a lot more of it. I don't get to give up after a really bad day. And I don't want to hurt you by not choosing you. I could never forgive myself."

Cori listened to her words very carefully, then made a split-second decision to stand up and remove her sweater and shirt. Standing there in just her spandex bra, she revealed the network of thin, light scars spread evenly across her torso and running down the length of her arms.

Aster looked understandably baffled.

"Before I attended college and started my medical training, I was a ground soldier in the Terran military in the war with Mars. These are scars from an involuntary cybernetic enhancement procedure to modify our bodies for combat with skeletal and muscular reinforcements for strength and agility, plus a neural implant to sync with our armor."

"You're from *Earth*?" Aster asked, blinking tears from her eyes.

Cori understood the reaction, to some extent. It was pretty rare to meet anyone from Earth, since the planet was mostly dead in the last few decades before its final destruction by the Martians, its population dwindling all through the relentless war. The ultimate loss of humans' ancestral homeworld sent shockwaves through their species, which she now knew as fact, though it was a specific form of grief she did not share.

"Yes. I was extremely lucky to be one of the few who were rescued before the planet was destroyed. I was seventeen at the time. When I was able to start over on Idun, I decided to devote the rest of my life to helping other people, in order to be worthy of that rescue. I'm telling you all this so you'll believe me when I say that I am not one to imagine rosy futures. I consider each new day a gift. I can also promise you right now that I'll *never* ask you to stop. I believe that you need the money, and that you've found the best way to get it."

With that, she pulled her top back on and returned to the sofa, closer now to Aster.

"What if our relationship wasn't like that, at all?" Cori asked. "What if you came home *here* after your work nights, and I healed you and then made you breakfast, and you could stay in and sleep instead of dealing with the clinic? What if we could see each other every day?"

Aster's smile trembled. "That sounds really nice."

"Please don't feel any pressure to decide right now if you need time to think it over," Cori went on, "but know that I'd really like to give this a chance. And I will *never* demand anything."

Aster pulled her into a swift hug, burying her face in her shoulder, and Cori rubbed her back. She couldn't be certain if this meant yes or no, but for the moment, she just held her.

All mystery evaporated when they were face-to-face again, noses nearly touching, and Aster leaned in to kiss her. Cori was suddenly frozen. Aster's lips were soft and delicate against hers in a way she had never properly imagined. For a moment, Cori was so stunned by the physical sensation that she forgot how to think or react in any way.

Fortunately, Aster didn't seem to notice. "I've wanted to do that for a while."

Cori smiled. "I'm glad you did."

Their lips met again. Cori focused this time, properly returning the affection as best as she could.

They remained on the sofa well into the night.

✳ ✳ ✳

Aster didn't have many things to pack the following day, mostly just clothes. Over her many nomadic years of moving from station to station, she had tried to avoid collecting much of anything. Closing up her suitcase, it still felt surreal to think that she was really doing this—moving out of the shabby little apartment she rented a year and a half ago ... and into her new girlfriend's apartment.

Cori was definitely full of surprises. Aster had never expected her to make such a *compelling* case for them to be together, with such a realistic and understanding approach to Aster's situation—one she planned to fully explain now, since she wanted Cori to know the truth.

But then, she also had never expected that her time on Victory would include meeting someone so wonderful, who—minor detail—was a refugee from fucking *Earth*. In hindsight, Cori's Common had always been a little *too* perfect, too polished, but Aster had assumed that was just an Idun thing.

Back when she was sixteen, the reports of the planet's destruction by the Martian military had affected Aster more than she thought it would. She hadn't anticipated feeling anything specific about a dead planet she'd only seen in photos, but the loss of Earth weighed heavily on her—and she wasn't alone in that. Entire books had been written about the collective experience of grief that accompanied the loss of the human species' origin planet. By the hands of other humans, no less.

Now able to enter Cori's apartment on her own, Aster was instantly bored and a little awkward in the empty room, so she changed into her athletic clothes and set out to find the gym. It turned out to be larger than the one at her old building, and with more options, so she did a few rounds on the arm and leg machines and then hit the treadmill for a long run, opting for a "cross-country" simulation that had her running through planetside wilderness.

It felt somewhat ironic that she was in the best shape of her life due to some rotten luck and a load of debt, but exercise had become more than just a way to stay strong and nimble. It was also how she cleared her mind and let herself forget everything else, at least for a couple hours, and focused on her own body and well-being. She was determined to emerge from the other side of this setback as a better, healthier version of herself.

Afterward, thoroughly spent and drenched in sweat, she showered and changed, combing out her wet hair and letting it air dry. She headed back to Cori's apartment, where she settled onto the sofa and munched on a nut bar. It still felt weird to be in the room alone, but now she was too tired to care as much.

Sometime later, after dozing off without realizing it, Aster woke to Cori touching her shoulder.

"Hi!" Aster said, sitting up.

"Hi," Cori said. They embraced and kissed on the sofa. "I've been looking forward to that."

Aster smiled. "Me, too."

"Just two bags?" Cori asked, gesturing toward Aster's suitcase and backpack.

"Yeah, I don't have much."

Cori's eyes sparkled with excitement. "Well, listen, there are a couple options here. I'm thinking I'll convert the spare room into a private exam room, so I'll have all the equipment I need to treat you right here."

"Is that...legal?" Aster asked. It felt like a silly question for Cori of all people, but she wanted to be sure.

"Oh, yes! Since I'm living in staff housing, I just have to register it as a private practice, and none of the equipment can leave the building. It's actually fairly common. Of course, if you ever have severe injuries, you can still go directly to the clinic."

Aster nodded. "No more parasites. Promise."

Cori gave her a curious look.

"I'm pretty sure I know how it happened," Aster explained. "A couple weeks ago, I went with a client back to their ship in the docks instead of a hotel room. I'll spare you the details of how not-clean it was, but I *must* have picked it up there, probably in larva form." She paused to shudder. "I shouldn't have gone there at all, but they were willing to pay a lot. Never again, obviously."

Cori touched her hand, looking sympathetic. "I'm sorry it had such awful consequences."

"So, something about options for the apartment?"

"Right, yes. If you want your own private space, that room could double as your bedroom, maybe with a curtain divider . . . Or, alternatively, you'd be welcome to stay with me, in the main bedroom. Whatever sounds most comfortable."

The thought of the two of them snuggled up together at night made Aster weak at the knees.

"Honestly," Aster said, "I kind of figured I'd be staying with you. If that's alright."

"Of course!" Cori said with a big smile. "If you change

your mind, though, don't hesitate to say so. We can always try something different."

"Sounds good, yeah."

With that settled, Aster kissed her again. Cori seemed eager enough that Aster wondered if they might end up in bed sooner rather than later, but Cori's hands stayed pretty chaste, never straying from her lower back.

"I'm so happy you're here," Cori said, stopping to look at her.

"So am I," Aster said. "Actually, now that we live together, I want to explain *why* I'm in debt. It's not exactly a flattering story, but I don't want to have this big secret from you."

"Okay," Cori said, warm and nonjudgmental as always.

Aster took a breath. "Nearly two years ago, when I was still station-hopping and taking odd jobs wherever I ended up, I fell in with a group of smugglers. I knew it was risky, but I figured it would be one job and then I'd never see them again. Their expected profit was just too good. The client was some government asshole, I guess, but I never actually saw them. Big jobs like that are highly competitive, and they normally require a contract of sorts—a safety net so that if the asset is lost, the smuggler crew has to pay up . . . and this particular job was a *massive* failure. Not only were the assets lost, but so was our ship, blown to bits, with everyone on board. Except for me, just by dumb luck, since I was out making repairs and my tether broke. So there I was, drifting in the void, watching one explosion after another.

I had plenty of oxygen, and I waited a couple hours to activate my distress beacon so that someone could scoop me up ... which they did."

Cori took Aster's hand and squeezed it. The gesture made her composure slip a little.

"So, you got stuck with the reimbursement for the client?" Cori asked.

Aster nodded. "I don't know how they found out I was alive, but they tracked me down pretty fast. I told them I had no way of paying that much, and they *helpfully* directed me to a broker here on Victory, who had a lender set up the funds and gave me five years to pay it back—five years before late fees kick in. If my income stays how it is now, I should be able to pay it off in *four* years and put it all behind me. So that's why I'm doing this. Because I'm not going to have this one fuck-up looming over me for the rest of my life. And I'm *not* going to burden my parents with it and hand them proof that I never should have left home. It's my mess, so I'm cleaning it up."

Cori shook her head. "What an awful situation."

"Yeah, but that's life sometimes. That broker guy offered to make me one of his cronies, hunting down people who haven't paid and pointing a gun in their face while their kids cry, to let me work off the debt that way. I said *no*. This work that I'm doing is my choice, and it's on my terms. The only person getting hurt is me. Plus, compared to the rest of that crew, I'm really fucking lucky. Since I'm alive."

"That's true," Cori agreed. "Can I ask what the asset was?"

"Oh, yeah, did I skip that? It was some old, dead ships, drifting out in neutral territory. We were just supposed to haul them over to a region where humans could 'legally' scoop them up. No idea what made them so special since somebody saw pirates and nuked everything."

"I see. Can I ask you something else?"

"Anything."

"You said *if* your income stays consistent, you'll get it paid off that timeframe. If something changes, do you have another plan?"

"Yeah," Aster said with a sigh. "If this place dries out or whatever, I'll go to a different station and find similar work. I'm hoping it won't come to that, though, since I have almost no competition out here."

"Well, I appreciate you explaining it to me. I'm sorry you're in such a difficult position, but I also admire your resilience."

"It actually feels good to tell someone everything . . . I haven't done that in a long time."

At their second dinner together, they fell into easy conversation about the books they were reading and new films they'd like to see. All the while, Aster was more than a little preoccupied by what might happen later. It had been a *long* time since she had been genuinely intimate with anyone, and she was vaguely lightheaded with anticipation. But maybe that was just the wine.

As they got ready for bed, Cori stepped out of the bathroom in her pajamas—a snug tank top and soft shorts—once again exposing the thin, light scars across her broad shoulders and long limbs alongside constellations of cute freckles. She'd always been pretty, but like this, she was *painfully* attractive. Aster started to wonder how she'd manage to sleep with someone so gorgeous right next to her. Damn, it really had been a long time.

After they settled into the nest of sheets, they were quickly kissing again. With their bodies close and hands exploring, and the scent of Cori's freshly showered skin, Aster lost herself to the feeling of being so enveloped. Just to be with her like this was more than she'd ever allowed herself to want.

But then, just like before, Cori stopped and looked at her. Her eyes were watery this time.

"Hey, what is it?" Aster asked, touching Cori's cheek.

"Sorry...I'm just happy. I hope that's not strange to say."

With a past partner, Aster might have bristled at the sentiment so early in their relationship, but Cori's earnestness was only endearing. She never wanted her to feel like she couldn't say what she was thinking.

"It's not strange at all. I'm happy, too. Happier than I've been in a long time."

They were still holding each other as they fell asleep.

6
Love Songs

In the days that followed Aster moving in, Cori was walking on air. She had never been so full of joy. A few lines from an ancient song kept dancing through her head—a wistful, romantic song by a singer asking her lover to run away together—even though she hadn't heard it in years.

It was so exciting to have something, *someone* to look forward to each day.

Near the end of her shift before her next free day, Cori was standing in the lobby when she glanced toward the courtyard, lined with vendors for the monthly pop-up market. That gave her an idea. Before heading back to her apartment, she went out to a flower cart and bought a bundle of pretty orange blooms. For a moment, she felt a little silly about it, but then something strange happened: As soon as she was holding the flowers and thinking of giving them to Aster, heat rushed to her cheeks.

How wonderful and weird romance was!

When she stepped through the door, Aster greeted her with a hug, and they kissed in exactly the way Cori had imagined all day.

"How was your day?" Aster asked.

"Oh, it was fine. These are for you."

"Oh," Aster said, taking the flowers with a little laugh. "Pretty! Thank you."

"From the market downstairs," Cori added. "I was just thinking about you, and—"

Aster kissed her again, cutting her off, and lingered, letting her hands run over Cori's back in a way that left Cori warm and dizzy. The idea of being physically intimate with Aster was deeply appealing, but Cori couldn't let herself dwell on it. She would never, ever rush this, nor behave in a way that might make Aster think she assumed they would do anything specific together.

"Thank you," Aster said again. "Really sweet of you. I've been thinking about you, too."

"It's been hard to think about anything else, to be honest."

"Same here. I have a surprise for you, too, actually. Dinner is almost ready, and I made one of my favorites from home."

"Oh, wow! I can't wait to try it."

They sat down to the single best meal Cori had since she'd come to Victory—a hearty squash lasagna that Aster remembered from childhood. Apparently, one of her mothers had imparted a love of cooking, particularly for shared meals. As they ate and talked, Aster also reached over to touch Cori's hand a few times, which was maybe even more wonderful than the food.

Afterward, when the table was clear, Cori pulled Aster into a grateful hug in the kitchen.

"Thank you. That was delicious."

"I'm glad you liked it."

Their next kiss was more ardent than before, Aster's hands lingering on Cori's hips. Pulse racing, Cori felt Aster's hand slip beneath her top, caressing her skin directly. The sensation made her gasp with an odd squeak that she didn't intend.

"Cori?" Aster asked, perhaps concerned.

"Sorry," she said with an awkward laugh. "I don't know why—"

"Do you *want* to do more than just kissing?"

The heat of one hundred suns rushed to her face. "Yes. If you do."

"Definitely," Aster said with a smile.

Cori was powerless to resist kissing her again.

"What do *you* like?" Cori asked, leaving out the part about how she had never done this before. Being open about her feelings had been so simple, but admitting her lack of experience was different. She would be totally honest if Aster asked her about it, but otherwise, she'd keep it to herself.

Cori didn't want Aster to feel any pressure to teach or guide her; she was pretty confident in her understanding of anatomy—and basic sexual techniques. But even more than that, she was eager to hear how Aster liked to be touched, because she'd never want to do it any other way.

In reply, though, Aster sighed, and her brow furrowed the slightest bit. "You know, I'm honestly not sure anymore?" The smile returned. "But I think I'd try anything with you."

Cori smiled back. "We'll figure it out together, then."

In bed moments later, Cori was trailing kisses down Aster's bare torso, slowly traveling lower. She had offered to pleasure her, and Aster had agreed, perhaps with some surprise. Cori was content to take the scenic route to the destination.

Placing a kiss beside Aster's navel, Cori looked up and found Aster watching her with hazy eyes and rosy cheeks, loose auburn waves falling around her face. She was as beautiful as a dream. Cori couldn't resist moving back up to her lips for one more kiss.

"Are you ready?" she asked.

Aster smiled. "Yes."

Trailing kisses down again, more rapidly this time, she moved to Aster's mons and pressed a slow kiss above the tuft of hair, hearing a breath hitch just after. Encouraged, Cori shifted lower, using two fingers and her tongue at once, as she'd read about. Her touch elicited a soft moan, so she repeated it with a little more force and felt Aster's hand take a firm grip of her shoulder.

Cori was able to find a good rhythm. All the while, Aster made the most wonderful sounds she'd ever heard. Cori had never been so aroused in her entire life; the feeling was both incredible and maddening, though she trained her focus on Aster's pleasure.

When she could tell that Aster was probably nearing her peak, she tried a new motion with her tongue, darting it quickly side to side.

"Fuck," Aster muttered, her chest heaving.

Cori's arousal had become distracting by that point, so without missing a beat, she slipped her hand into her own pants and swiftly brought herself to climax with a few efficient rubs. She sighed against Aster as she came, unsure if she noticed, then resumed her prior focus, glad of the renewed mental clarity.

Moments later, Aster cried out in a higher pitch as she came, and the sound gave way to a breathy laugh as her body relaxed. After pressing a final kiss to her inner thigh, Cori moved up to lie beside her, finding Aster rosy-cheeked and glowing.

Aster quickly pulled her into a happy kiss. "Want me to return the favor?"

"Oh," Cori said, regretful—she should have anticipated that offer. "Maybe next time? I actually finished already, too."

"Oh," Aster echoed, eyebrows shooting up in surprise. "Alright."

"I really enjoyed that," Cori added.

"Me, too," Aster replied with a small chuckle. "That was . . . well, you're good at it."

"I'm glad you think so."

✳ ✳ ✳

After a longer break than usual, Aster had reached the point where she couldn't keep putting off going out for a work night. She *normally* worked three or four nights per week, ideally not in a row, in order to allow herself the space to recuperate physically and mentally afterward. With the parasite incident still fresh on her mind, she was more anxious than usual, but the best way forward was to get it over with.

First, there was the prep: a single shot of alcohol to loosen her muscles. Never more than that, since she needed her mind to stay sharp. Next, she dressed in one of several ridiculous ensembles that had been proven to attract the right attention—she chose a skintight gold unitard under an iridescent chainmail dress and tall violet boots. Very sparkly, very human-shaped.

For her face, she applied purple lipstick and flared white eyeliner, then turned up her head and used cosmetic eye drops to turn her blue irises temporarily bright yellow, creating a fiery look alongside her auburn hair. As a finishing touch, she dusted a fine, semi-luminescent glitter over her cheekbones—a product designed to shine bright in dark dance clubs.

It wasn't her style, but she had to admit that it wasn't a *terrible* look. Maybe in some other life she could have worn this to go out partying.

Just then, she heard Cori returning from work.

"Aster?"

"I'm in here," she answered. "I'm dressed for work, so . . . try not to faint." Stepping out, she found Cori in the bedroom.

"Wow, you look . . . different!" Cori raised her eyebrows in surprise.

"I know," Aster laughed. "It's wild. It's supposed to make me stand out."

"The makeup is so interesting," Cori said, stepping closer. "I haven't seen that before."

"No, I always wash up and change before the clinic . . . And I *probably* should have waited to put this on so that you could touch my face. Sorry."

"Oh, no worries," Cori said, reaching out and taking her hand. "Do you need anything before you go?"

"No, I'm all set."

"Okay. Well, I'll see you when you get back!"

It was a nice thought, coming back here when she was finished, even though it was a bit nerve-wracking to be putting Cori's plan into play. Her last partner had been too disgusted to stick around longer than a month after Aster started escorting, and his words still lingered in her mind: *How could you let them touch you like that? I can't even look at you.*

But Cori *wasn't* him. She was a better person in every way. Aster felt safe with her. She had to let herself trust that if this relationship had any chance of working.

As she climbed the stairs at the train platform, she passed a group of people in scarlet uniforms: sex workers from the pleasure center. She looked away, but she could feel the angry glances. She understood their point of view—she should get a *real job,* like them, instead of working cross-species and making escorts and all other humans look bad in the process.

The zones on the outer rim of the central hub were popular with non-humans. As Aster rode the train to her usual stop, she tried to clear her mind. The space bug was an outlier. This would be a normal night, she told herself. One of hundreds. So average it would fade from memory with time.

As she started down the familiar avenues with their garish glowing signs, nightclubs blaring shitty voidsynth "music," and a myriad of weird smells, she found the streets crowded, which was good. She rarely had to walk far before catching someone's eye—some alien traveler on a stopover, feeling brave or bored enough to try something exotic.

On the next block, she got the sense that someone was

following her and confirmed with a quick glance that she was being trailed by an interested customer—an Orykter, standing taller than her, with large, pointed ears and a long, slender snout. Aster had been with quite a few of them; they tended to be very interested in humans. She could tell this one might be a bit shy, so she ducked into an alley and waited for them to follow or change their mind.

The Orykter appeared beside her moments later. Her name was Riinari, and Aster could tell she was new to this and a bit nervous. She only spoke a little Common, and Aster spoke almost no Oryktiin; the single word she could articulate perfectly across multiple alien languages was "stop." While Riinari read an auto-translation on her comm, Aster gave her rate for one hour and explained how the process would work: A half payment now and then a walk to a nearby motel, where rooms were rentable from an automated kiosk, followed by the other half payment as soon as they were in private. That seemed to put the client more at ease, since she requested Aster's account number and eagerly submitted the first payment.

Aster didn't have rosy thoughts about her clients, but she also didn't resent them. She viewed each session as a simple transaction: She needed money, and these individuals were willing to pay for something she was willing to offer. It was just work, and people had done some version of this work for most of human history—people in far more dangerous conditions, without access to modern healing technology.

Alicia Haberski

✹ ✹ ✹

By the time Aster headed home, in the early morning when the crowds had thinned, she remained uninjured and had a hefty profit in her account. The only soreness was her scalp, where her long hair had been tugged repeatedly by her second client. She rubbed it with both hands as she rode the elevator to Cori's apartment.

When Aster stepped inside, she found Cori awake and waiting.

"Hi," Cori said, in greeting as much as in question.

"I'm fine. I just need to wash up."

"Good. I left a robe for you."

After scrubbing herself clean under the hot water, Aster pulled her wet hair into a drying cloth and donned the soft green robe Cori had set out. When she emerged from the bathroom, she found Cori still waiting. They embraced and kissed before settling into bed. With Cori's arms snugly around her, Aster was swiftly asleep.

When Aster heard Cori's alarm a couple hours later, it was like only minutes had passed. She felt Cori press a kiss to her cheek before she got up to get ready for work. Aster really wanted to keep sleeping, but she *was* hungry, so she forced herself to get up and have breakfast with Cori.

"Are you exhausted?" Aster asked as they ate sliced fruit and toast.

Cori looked confused. "No?"

"You didn't have to stay up and wait for me."

"Oh! I didn't. I was asleep on the couch until I heard you get back."

"Oh." Aster blinked. "You . . . the couch is comfortable enough?"

Cori shrugged. "Yeah, I can sleep anywhere. How are you?"

"Fine. Better now."

"Good," Cori said with a warm smile.

When Cori was dressed and ready to go downstairs, Aster pulled her into a long kiss.

Afterward, Cori gave her a look of tender regret. "I do wish I could just stay in bed with you."

"I know. I'll see you later."

"Already looking forward to it."

Aster went back to bed and slept until midday, waking up free from the looming pressure of a work night. She couldn't resist a trip to her favorite dumpling shop for lunch, even though it now meant a train ride.

In her old zone, she sat on a bench to eat, with a view of the intersection where Cori had caught the falling post—still lying off to the side of the road. Two kids were walking across it with their arms out for balance; one of them wavered, making the other one laugh and tumble off. She couldn't help but laugh with them.

Aster was always in a better mood on days like this, but

today she felt happier than she had in ages. Maybe Victory wasn't such a shithole after all.

✳ ✳ ✳

When evening rolled around and Cori was back in the apartment, Aster greeted her with a kiss the second she came through the door.

"Hi," Cori said just after.

"Hi."

As they kissed again, it was obvious that they were equally happy to see each other. But Cori seemed to be holding back. To reassure her, Aster moved to press a kiss to her jaw and let her hands settle on Cori's hips. There was nothing she'd like more than to be touched by someone she was genuinely excited to be with.

"It's not too soon?" Cori asked, breathless.

"Not for me," Aster replied. "I'm perfectly fine."

With that settled, they fell quickly into bed, tearing at each other's clothes this time. Aster welcomed the new enthusiasm, pulling Cori close and kissing her after they were nude.

Relishing the warmth of Cori's skin, Aster ran her fingers up Cori's thigh and thought she felt a little tremble in response.

"Would you want to ... touch each other this time?"

Instead of answering, Cori looked suddenly frozen.

"Never mind if you don't want—" Aster started, moving her hand back to Cori's waist.

"No! It's not that. I do. I do want. Just . . . you're sure you're not sore at all? I wouldn't want to make it worse."

Aster suddenly understood the hesitation. "Oh, no, I'm not . . . they don't all touch me like that. Some do, but others are . . . different. They don't always want sex—or a human version of it. Sorry, I'm being vague on purpose. I don't want to spoil the mood."

Cori touched her cheek. "You can tell me anything."

"I mostly don't want to talk about it."

"That's fine, too."

"What I do want," Aster said, pressing another kiss to her lips, "is for both of us to have a nice time."

Cori sighed into the kiss in a soft, delicate way, pulling Aster closer to her body, apparently eager to agree.

✷ ✷ ✷

Cori was happy to let Aster take the lead as they got situated. She quickly found that even the slightest touch of Aster's hand between her legs was enough to have her seeing stars and making all sorts of embarrassing sounds she'd never heard emerge from her mouth before. It was so different from touching herself, so much more *electric,* that she felt like her head was spinning.

The first time Aster slipped a finger inside, Cori gasped

in a way that was so utterly ridiculous, she half expected to hear Aster laugh after. Instead, she kissed her neck and repeated the same wonderful motion with her hand.

That was all the prompting Cori needed to catch up. She found that touching Aster in a similar way elicited the same incredible sounds from the first time they'd been together— and now she could also see the way Aster bit her bottom lip and tipped her head back.

They fell into a rhythm together, alternating the give and receive as though it was a song they were learning together. A song of celebration. In a fleeting moment of reflection, Cori wondered how often making love felt like making art. Like an act of profound and timeless beauty. Maybe the difference wasn't really that significant.

It didn't take long for Cori to reach her peak.

"Ah, fuck!" she blurted in surprise. "That was quick— I didn't even think I was about to—"

Aster smiled at that, panting. "It's been a while for me, too."

Her eyes sparkled in the lamplight beneath her glorious mess of auburn waves. All Cori could do was admire her for a moment.

"You are *so* beautiful," she said, the word wholly inadequate to describe Aster.

"So are you," Aster said, raising up to bring their lips together.

Cori moved back into place, happy to give Aster her

undivided attention—and quietly triumphant when Aster cried out even louder with her own orgasm.

Lying in the afterglow, Cori admired the tattoos on the back of Aster's arm, where she hadn't looked closely before. She ran her fingers over a likeness of Earth after the image rotated to show all continents and then went still again.

"Is that one ridiculous to you?" Aster asked.

"Not at all. It's important to remember our past. Especially our tendency toward the destruction of beautiful things. Not that the planet was ever *beautiful* when I saw it. But once, long before, in the old pictures."

"Is that why you kept these?" Aster asked, turning and running her fingers along the thin scars on Cori's chest. "To remember?"

Cori nodded. "That, and I'm used to them. They look familiar in the mirror even when other things change. I never knew how my hair would look until it started growing out."

Aster reached out to run her hand over Cori's light locks. "And now it's perfect."

Cori laughed a little at that, amused by the thought of her hair being called *perfect* next to Aster's.

"I mean it. You're stunning, Cori. I've thought so since we met."

Cori's heart did a little flip. She was pretty neutral about her own appearance, but hearing those words from Aster was surprisingly moving. "Likewise."

Aster pulled her close, resting their foreheads together. They lay in silence for a while before she spoke again.

"What are the chances? That our paths would cross?"

"Immeasurably small," Cori said softly. "But nothing so wonderful is ever probable."

7
Oasis

The next time Aster went out for work, she returned in rough shape.

Cori snapped awake on the sofa when she heard the door lock disengage. She stepped over just in time for Aster to stumble into her, grasping her shoulders for support.

"I've got you," Cori said. "Where are you hurt?"

"It's my hip...area," she explained, catching her breath.

"Okay. Let's get you into bed."

"Wait. I want to shower first."

"Aster, you can barely stand."

"I always bathe first. I want to be clean."

"Okay," Cori said, relenting. "I'll help you get undressed."

After Aster shed her clothes, Cori could see significant bruising on her pelvis and wondered if the damage was worse than she realized.

"Careful," she said, supporting her as she stepped into the shower.

"I'm okay. This is the easy part."

Her tone was calm and reassuring, but Cori was still concerned as she stepped away from the bathroom. To occupy her time, she went into the treatment room and activated the lights, setting out a few pieces of equipment and making sure everything was in order.

She heard the water cut off and hurried back to the bathroom, where she found Aster pulling on the green robe while keeping her weight on one foot.

"Here," Cori said, bending down a bit, "put your arms around me and I'll carry you."

Aster did so, and Cori gently lifted her, supporting her torso and taking her to the treatment room so that Aster didn't have to walk anymore. When Cori reached the bed and eased her down, Aster winced.

"How bad is the pain?"

"Uh, moderate," Aster said, brow furrowed.

Cori administered two doses of AnoDyn, then pulled the robe partly open and took some scans. As it turned out, Aster's hip was inflamed, but the more serious damage was nearby—a hairline fracture in her pelvis.

"This will take some time," she said, getting the healing lamp calibrated. "Feel free to sleep. And let me know if you need anything."

"I'm fine; just tired," Aster said. She dozed off shortly after the lamp went to work.

Cori stayed by her side all the while, glad that Aster was home and safe and getting her undivided attention. The thought of her having to cope with so many injuries alone for so long weighed heavily on Cori's heart.

When the machine beeped its completion, Cori removed it and rescanned. Aster opened her hazy eyes.

"Halfway there," Cori said. "Now I'll get your hip taken care of."

She recalibrated the machine and reset it over the hip joint, which wouldn't take as long, then turned her attention back to Aster, who gave her a lazy smile. Cori smiled back, though she hoped Aster wouldn't mind the semi-awkward question she would need to ask soon.

The lamp beeped once again, and Cori moved to retrieve it, rescanning to confirm the hip was fully healed. Next, she took up a salve.

"I'll apply this to the bruising, if that's alright."

Aster nodded.

Cori carefully spread it over each dark spot, making sure not to press too hard, then met Aster's gaze again, keeping her expression neutral.

"Based on your injuries, I take it this client preferred the human version of sex?"

Aster looked at the ceiling and responded with a tiny nod.

"With your consent, I'll examine your pelvic area as well."

"*Pelvic area,*" Aster repeated in an odd tone.

Cori hated making her so uncomfortable, and she realized that the strictly medical approach might be all wrong. Moving over to Aster's face, she touched her shoulder.

"I'm sorry. I know this isn't fun. If you don't have any discomfort there, I don't need to look."

Aster sighed. "You should check."

After giving her shoulder a squeeze, Cori returned to the end of the bed and used a light to fully examine her externally. She found some additional inflammation and bruising that warranted a second salve, which she applied with Aster's permission.

"I can reapply that for you later, or you can do it yourself. It should feel better soon."

"Yeah, I've used that kind before. I normally do it myself."

"Oh, good. Alright."

She helped Aster into a sitting position, and they embraced.

"Don't be afraid to tell me about anything that hurts, okay? I want to help you."

"I know," Aster said. "Just getting used to this. First time's always the weirdest, right?"

Cori hesitated a moment. "Well, yes. Of course."

"I mean, I *know* you've seen everything already," Aster added. "But first time in a *medical* setting."

Cori glanced to the side, opening her mouth to speak but still working out the right words to say.

"Wait. Did you already—? *When?*"

"After I removed the parasite," Cori said, feeling suddenly guilty. "I checked for external damage, just to be sure."

At that, Aster's smile went crooked, and she barked an odd laugh, cupping a hand over her mouth.

"Sorry if that's uncomfortable to know—"

"No," Aster said, still laughing. "It's not that! It's fine. I was just . . . I was just lying here hoping that you'd still be attracted to me after this, but that *clearly* wasn't an issue after you fished a space bug out of my guts!"

She laughed again as if that statement were deeply hilarious. Cori was happy to see her spirits lifted.

"That's definitely *never* going to be an issue," she said, pecking Aster's cheek.

Cori had just enough time for breakfast before she needed to get ready for work. When she was dressed, Aster pulled her into a goodbye hug. "Are you going to be alright on low sleep?"

"Oh, absolutely," Cori said, wholly unconcerned. "I've been awake for upwards of fifty hours without getting foggy. Not that it was *fun*."

"Wow. Well, I hope you have a good day. I'll see you later."

"I'm already looking forward to it."

As she took the elevator down to the clinic, Cori found comfort in the mental image of Aster safe and cozy in bed—much better than wondering if she were alright, or when Cori would see her again. Yes, this arrangement was superior in every way.

✹ ✹ ✹

One of Aster's favorite parts of living with Cori was waking up together on a day when Cori wasn't working and just staying in bed for a while.

On mornings like this, the room felt like the only place on the station that really mattered. Nothing that happened outside of here was really important compared to the way Cori's eyes crinkled when she smiled, or the pillow creases on her cheek.

"Hey, can I ask you something?"

Aster nodded. "Anything."

Cori raised up on her elbow, her uncombed hair sticking up in random places. "It's okay if you hate this idea, but I've been thinking . . . maybe we could go out to dinner sometime? I could take you on a real date."

"Oh," Aster said in surprise.

"No pressure if it would be too stressful for you. I just think it might be fun. Sometime." She punctuated that statement with a kiss to Aster's shoulder and relaxed into the bed again.

It did make sense that Cori wanted to get out more; they'd been spending nearly all their free time in her apartment. And the thought of the two of them dressed up for date night *did* actually sound fun.

"Sure. Let's do it."

"Really?" Cori asked, eyes wide.

Aster laughed. "Yeah. It can be an experiment."

"Exactly!" Cori said, clearly excited. "If it's not fun for you, we won't do it again."

"Oh... that's not the experimental part to me, but sure."

Cori smiled and kissed her. Aster figured this could play out two ways: The outing would be fine, in which case she was overly paranoid, or it would backfire somehow, in which case she would have proof that she was *not* overly paranoid.

Either way, they'd have a good meal.

She chose a restaurant called Cafe Oasis, one of the better places, food-wise, even if the decor was cheesy and dated.

It was clear that neither of those words occurred to Cori, though, because when they entered and she saw the pillars made to look like trees, the ceiling painted as a cloudy blue sky, and the green "grass" carpet underfoot, all against the sound of recorded birdsong, she seemed genuinely charmed.

"This is so neat," she remarked as they were guided to their table. "Like we're on a picnic!"

Aster just smiled, keeping her thoughts to herself.

When they were seated across from each other in a cozy booth under warm lamplight, Cori beamed. She noticed the wall beside them, decorated to look like a trellis covered in flowering vines—the boards cracked and crumbling, and the cloth flowers faded with age.

"How cute," she said, reaching out to touch it, then thinking better of that choice.

"I'm glad you like it. Hopefully the food doesn't disappoint."

"Oh, I'm sure it won't if you liked it before!"

"Well, it *has* been a while," Aster said.

Once they had their drinks, a small group was seated nearby, and Aster awkwardly eyed them, thinking that one looked like a pleasure center worker she had seen before, but maybe not.

"Hey," Cori said, reaching across the table and taking her hand. "Don't think about anyone but me, okay? I'm happy we're here. You look beautiful."

Aster nodded again and squeezed her hand, but as the evening progressed, that proved to be easier said than done. By the time they were eating, every table around them was occupied by lively guests, and Aster couldn't shake the feeling that *someone* in here would recognize her in a bad way.

"Now *this* is delicious," Cori remarked about her pasta, oblivious. "I can see why this is a popular place!"

A server passed by their table with a couple of guests;

one of them doubled back to face them—a tall man who seemed vaguely familiar.

"Good evening, Dr. Nova," he said.

"Oh! Good evening, Director Davis," Cori replied, professional as ever. "What a welcome coincidence."

Aster froze, her heart rate doubling. This was the same director she had heard berating Cori for the parasite incident, she knew. And now Cori was dining with the same *hooker* who caused so much trouble.

"I see you've discovered one of my favorite places on Victory."

"Ah, yes! We're having a wonderful meal. This is Aster—Aster, Director Davis is the Head of Human Health on Victory."

Aster looked up, reluctantly, and managed to blurt, "Nice to meet you."

"Likewise." For a fleeting moment, he gave her a curious look, then returned his attention to Cori. "Well, I'll let you get back to your meal. Have a nice evening."

"Thank you," Cori said with a smile.

Just like that he was gone, and Aster could feel herself coming down from that colossal stress spike.

"Arrogant asshole," Cori muttered, taking a long sip of her drink.

"I . . . couldn't tell if he recognized me," Aster said.

"Oh? Have you met him before?"

"No," Aster said, seeing Cori's brow crease with

confusion. "But he could have seen me in passing... or remembered my name?"

Cori waved her hand. "Well, don't worry about him. He's been playing nice ever since 3H requested me."

Aster sighed, twisting her napkin in her lap. She would like to brush off the encounter so easily, but the idea that the director might know about Cori's relationship status and use it against her had her stomach in knots.

"Is your food alright?" Cori asked.

"It's fine. But he's the one who hired you, right? The same director who Dr. Rylen reported to?"

Cori set down her fork and reached out for Aster's hand again. "Listen—"

She was interrupted by yet another person standing beside the table. This time it was a young woman with glowing raver tattoos and complicated face jewelry.

"Sorry to interrupt," she said. "But did you say... you're Dr. Nova?"

"That's right," she answered cheerfully.

"My brother saw you a while back. He works in the docks and got his hand crushed. He was afraid it would never work again. But you fixed it perfectly... I just wanted to thank you in person."

"Oh, I remember him well," Cori said with an earnest fondness. "I'm so glad I was able to help. Your thanks isn't necessary, but it is appreciated."

After the woman had gone, Cori gave Aster a look. "I think my reputation is secure with the people who matter."

✳ ✳ ✳

It wasn't until they were back at their apartment that Aster realized something: When she was out with Cori, she *wasn't* an escort. She was a *doctor's* partner. That was a nice thought.

Another nice thought was that Aster had fully recovered from her most recent work night, which meant they could be intimate again.

"That was fun," Cori said, pulling her into a kiss in their apartment. "Thank you for indulging me."

"Of course. I'm glad you liked it. Sorry for being paranoid."

"Always looking out for me," Cori said, stroking her jaw. "First time is always weird, right?"

Aster snort-laughed at that reference. "*Wow.*"

It wasn't long before they were in bed, Cori trailing kisses across Aster's bare chest—far more eagerly than she had in the past. That made Aster smile.

When Cori moved to kiss her lips again, Aster felt bold enough to take hold of Cori's hips and pull her closer, letting her settle between her legs, hoping she'd take the cue.

Cori hesitated. "Your . . . hip isn't still sore?"

Aster blinked. "No? That was last week. Ancient history."

Cori still looked unsure. "Okay. Please tell me if it ever feels—"

"I will," Aster said. "I promise. Don't worry about that, okay? I wouldn't ask you to do anything that didn't feel good."

Cori nodded and pressed a kiss to her cheek as she began rocking against her. Aster hummed, holding her close.

Aster had never been with anyone like Cori. The way she made love was absent of any ego, any desire to impress, and purely about celebrating each other. She held Aster like she was something precious, kissed her skin like she was savoring it. And every time their eyes met, Aster found pure adoration there.

Aster didn't need to hear Cori say it to know that she loved her. With someone else, that might have been too intense, but with Cori, it made Aster want to hold on and never let go.

8
Perspective

One morning, after leaving Aster cozy in bed, Cori was greeted by a patient case that gave her immediate flashbacks: It was a young man named Tymon with a cracked rib and a sprained ankle. Cori couldn't help but recall Aster's appointments for those same injuries, but she cleared her head as she stepped into the exam room.

Her heart sank to see him: He was covered in suction-cup bruising and visibly shaken.

After introducing herself and administering pain meds, Cori sat with him while multiple healing lamps went to work. "Let me know if you feel any discomfort."

"Thank you," he said. "And thank you for . . . being so nice."

"Of course, Tymon. I'm here to help you."

"I messed up," he mumbled. "I shouldn't have gone there—but I—"

His heart rate jumped, so Cori placed a hand on his forearm to ground him. "You needed the money, right?"

He nodded, sadly.

"Listen," she said. "You're going to be fine. Everything that happened is behind you, and you get to move forward from here."

"I'll *never* do that again," he said with conviction. "Never."

"I'm glad to hear it. But please don't hesitate to come back and see me if you ever need to."

After the session was complete, Cori sent him off with a salve for the bruises, then found herself wondering what Aster's first-ever work night must have been like. How badly was she hurt that time? How awful was it to know that she had no end in sight?

Back in their apartment that evening after her shift, Cori pulled Aster into a very long hug.

"Hi," Aster said happily. "Long day?"

"Somewhat," Cori replied with a shrug. "Oh, I do need to ask you something."

"Hmm?"

"Later this week there's going to be a party for the medical staff. Everyone can bring their partners. Would you want to go with me and meet some of my coworkers? I mean, no pressure. I know it doesn't sound exciting."

"Sure," Aster said. "If you want me to come, I'm in."

"Of course I do!" Cori hugged her again.

With that settled, they spent a relaxing evening together, having dinner and watching a few serial episodes while snuggling. Cori relished evenings like this one, when they could fully unwind and enjoy each other's company, knowing that they were both in for the night, and then fall asleep next to each other.

Up close, she also noticed that a dark bruise on the side of Aster's neck hadn't faded at all.

"Have you used any salve on this one?" Cori asked, wishing a second later that she hadn't mentioned it—she had been trying to reserve medical talk for the treatment room, as much as possible.

"Oh ... I forgot about that one, actually. It doesn't feel like anything."

Cori pressed a kiss to her cheek. "Never mind, then."

✴ ✴ ✴

Aster was more than a little nervous as she got dressed for Cori's work party.

The thought of mingling with a bunch of doctors was pretty daunting, but at least Aster hadn't been a regular patient at *this* clinic. There was still a tiny part of her brain that felt like this could backfire on Cori, somehow, but she was better at ignoring that paranoia these days. They'd gone out several times now, to restaurants and the cinema, and nothing bad had happened. So Aster wasn't going to decline an invitation to meet the other medical staff. Even if her hands were clammy as she pulled on one of her dressier jackets to hide the purple blotches lingering on her arms.

She was meeting Cori at the event, in a private party room of a restaurant on the lowest floor of the hospital. When she arrived, she found the room set up with light refreshments and tables scattered beneath a wall projection that read *Thank You 3H Staff*.

"Aster!" Cori said, appearing beside her. "You look beautiful!"

Aster smiled; Cori had seen the jacket plenty of times. "Thank you."

"I'm glad you're here," Cori said, touching her arm.

They were greeted by an older woman with short dark hair and kind eyes, whom Cori introduced as Dr. Kalani LaRue, the head physician at this clinic. After she had moved on, Cori privately shared that she was the best of the bunch and the exact opposite of Dr. Davis.

A flurry of more introductions followed, with Cori greeting and briefly chatting with several other doctors and nurses. The way they all carried on, Aster could imagine that Cori had been here for years instead of months.

"Cori, this is Dr. Dmitry Ramos, from 2H," Dr. LaRue said at one point, introducing a younger man. "I don't think you've met."

"Ah, we haven't!" Cori confirmed. "Nice to meet you, Dr. Ramos."

"Likewise," he said. "You transferred from 4H, is that right?"

"That's right," Dr. LaRue replied before Cori could speak. "She performed that alien parasite removal in 4H—we snatched her up right after."

Aster hoped that her face didn't give away the jolt of pure shock that slammed through her at the mention of that surgery.

"Oh my stars!" Dr. Ramos exclaimed, eyes wide. "You're a *legend*!"

There was a pause before Cori responded. "I didn't realize word had spread so far."

"Is it true," someone else interjected, "that you insisted on performing the surgery yourself, even though 4H wasn't fully equipped for the procedure?"

"Well, yes," Cori said. "There was no time to spare for the patient in question. It was the only possible choice."

"And the parasite had *never* been seen in a human before?" yet another voice asked.

Aster had stopped looking at their faces.

"Not to my knowledge," Cori answered politely. "I think the bio-analyst had an exciting day."

Polite laughter followed. A small group had clustered around them. Aster had absolutely no idea that Cori was *famous* for what she had done to save her life. Although the discussion was a bit surreal, her heart swelled with pride to know that her partner was such a star among other doctors.

"What did it look like? How did it enter the body?" came another eager questioner.

"Prostitution, wasn't it?" someone farther away offered.

"It was ... blue," Cori said. "Roughly the size of my hand. Not like anything I'd seen before. I didn't take a long look. I was just glad the patient arrived in time for me to help them. I'm sure any one of us would have made the same call."

"Don't be so humble, Dr. Nova!" Dr. LaRue said with a hand-wave. "It's not every day that we have an emergency eleven-hour surgery to remove a *live* alien parasite—with a happy ending, no less. We were *all* talking about it when we heard."

It wasn't really that long, Aster thought, glancing at Cori's face. *Was it?*

"Eleven hours," a younger doctor echoed. "Was anything in there *not* damaged?"

"It was extensive," Cori confirmed. "The nursing team at 4H did an excellent job keeping up with me after such a long shift—due to the engineering explosion."

A chorus of gasps followed, but Aster didn't hear the next few questions because she was too busy trying not to crumple to the floor. *Eleven hours.* She knew the surgery was complicated, but she had never even thought to ask how long it took.

"And the patient made a *full* recovery?"

"Yes," Cori said more warmly, "I'm happy to say they did."

"It was me," Aster chimed in, lifting her head and swallowing. "I was the patient. And yes, I'm fully recovered, all thanks to her."

Abruptly, the group went quiet. Cori looked at her and touched her arm.

"She did the hard work," Cori said. "Holding on the whole time."

"My apologies, Aster," Dr. LaRue said. "If I had known—"

"It's okay. I don't mind talking about it. I wouldn't be standing here if it weren't for her."

There was a brief moment of silence as people took awkward sips of their drinks. Maybe she shouldn't have said anything, she thought. Maybe she should have just let them do doctor talk. Cori took her hand and squeezed it.

"You knew each other," someone piped up, "before the surgery?"

"We did," Cori answered. "Aster was already a friend."

"What was going through your mind?" Dr. Ramos asked Aster directly.

She met his gaze. "I was ... really scared. I've never been so scared in my whole life. But she told me I would live, and I believed her."

✳ ✳ ✳

A while later, they managed to escape from the party and

found solitude in the elevator on the way back to their apartment. Aster swiftly pulled Cori into a firm embrace, now that they were finally alone.

"I'm so sorry," Cori said. "I had no idea when I dragged you here that anyone would want to talk about that surgery."

"No, Cori . . . it's okay," Aster said, her voice catching. "I'm so proud of you. I never realized how exceptional it was."

Cori held her gaze, giving her a fond smile. "It didn't feel exceptional to me. It was just what I needed to do. I'm glad I was there when it happened."

At their floor, Aster walked down the hall in a daze. She had always known that Cori was a gifted doctor, but hearing the way the others praised her—and wanted to learn from her—was a whole new perspective.

Back in their apartment with her jacket shed, Aster pulled Cori into her arms once more, kissing her deeply and then pulling back to look at her.

"What is it?" Cori asked. She really didn't get it.

"I had no idea it took eleven hours," Aster said, swallowing. "How ridiculous that I brought you a box of fruit after that."

"No," Cori said with a sad laugh, "not ridiculous. I was very touched that you came to see me."

When Aster kissed her again, she didn't stop, running her hands over Cori's back and moving to lift up her top. It had been a while, and Aster was very much ready to take her girlfriend to bed.

"Wait," Cori said, suddenly serious. "You're not fully healed."

I don't care, Aster wanted to say. She knew Cori meant well, but lately she kept feeling like she had to *convince* Cori to be intimate with her.

"I'm fine," Aster said, shaking her head. "I'm not sore at all."

Cori still looked hesitant. Uncomfortable, even.

"Wait," Aster said, backing off. "If you don't *want* to, that's fine . . . I mean, if I'm initiating too often—"

"Oh gosh, no," Cori said, brow furrowed. "It's not that. I don't mean to give you that impression."

"Then what?"

"It's just that . . . you've been through so much pain already. I can't be the reason there's more."

"Cori," Aster scolded, "I told you not to worry about that. Being with you isn't anything like my work—it's basically the opposite."

"I'm glad . . . But you've told me how many of your injuries happen by accident, because the clients are stronger than you? And I am *also* much stronger than you. More than you may realize."

Aster gave her a look. "Strong enough to catch a falling post."

"You saw that?"

Aster nodded and touched her cheek, looking into her big, pretty eyes. How could she make Cori understand that she felt completely safe with her? "I trust you. And you can trust *me*, too. I'll be honest if anything is ever too much. I won't let you do something you'll regret."

Cori responded by pulling Aster into a gentle embrace. Aster hugged her back—tight.

"Please don't ever think I want less of you," Cori said softly, shifting to look at her again. "That couldn't be further from the truth."

Aster grabbed her in reply, crashing their mouths together. Cori returned the affection, running her hands over her waist and up her back. Aster's head was abruptly swimming with anticipation.

Cori had always been gentle, but this time, she was even more so, and they took it more slowly than usual. As Cori undressed her, she pressed her lips to each expanse of skin, avoiding the lingering bruises. When they were finally in bed, Cori dipped to meet her lips for a long kiss and then trailed more kisses along her jaw and up to her ear, smelling her hair just after—as she often did.

Cori might have been a warrior once, but Aster couldn't imagine her being violent. Not when every way she caressed and moved and kissed was so deeply kind and loving.

Lying together afterward in comfortable silence, Aster's thoughts drifted between the things she'd learned at the party, to the old bed she slept in alone for so long, and to what Cori had said once before about their chances of meeting being *immeasurably small*. Aster had spent so much time cursing her luck and wishing she could go back in time and not be stupid enough to take that smuggling job. But now, things had changed. Now, it was hard to be mad about ending up here anymore—because *here* meant being in bed with Cori.

"What's going on in there?" Cori asked, brushing a stray lock of hair away from Aster's temple.

Aster smiled. "Just thinking... I haven't been lucky in a long time. So maybe this is the universe balancing out. Or something like that."

"I feel very lucky, too," Cori said fondly.

Aster curled into her, wishing she could stay there forever. Wishing they could both be this happy all the time, and thinking that maybe one day they would be.

9
Wounds

Aster stumbled into the elevator at their building and sank to her knees. She tried to take a deep breath to calm herself and failed when a flash of pain shot through her chest.

When she opened her eyes, she realized she was bleeding on the floor. She should *probably* go to the clinic in this state, she knew. But she really didn't want to. She wanted to be home with Cori and avoid having to explain herself to strangers after one of the most humiliating moments of her life.

When the doors opened on her floor, she pulled herself upright and shambled down the hall.

"Oh no," Cori said at the door, helping her inside. "What happened?"

Aster collapsed into her, catching her breath.

"It wasn't the client," she managed.

"What?" Cori asked. "Who did this?"

"At the train platform... on the stairs. Someone tripped me. I don't know who it was. I fell hard. I would have been *fine* if they hadn't fucking done that."

"Oh, Aster, I'm so sorry. Do you want to take a shower?"

Aster shook her head. She was in too much pain this time.

"Okay, let's get you into bed. You'll be alright."

In the treatment room, Cori scooped her up and lifted her onto the bed.

"My ribs are the worst, I think," she said. "Hurts to breathe."

"Here comes the AnoDyn." Aster felt the pinch of three quick stamps on her arm. Within seconds, her pain melted away and she relaxed into the bed. The tears she had been holding back fell freely in relief.

"I'll get a full body scan to be sure your ribs are the worst of it," Cori said, petting her head. "You can sleep now. I'm sorry this happened."

Aster felt a kiss on her cheek just before she drifted into a dreamless sleep. Sometime later, she became aware of Cori helping her reposition in bed but sleep quickly overtook her once again.

When she fully woke up, she had no concept of how much time had passed—except that she was now in the bedroom with Cori lying beside her.

"Welcome back," Cori said, stroking her arm.

"Did you finish already?"

"Yes, hours ago. You were responding to me when I carried you in here, but you did seem groggy. I'm glad you were able to rest."

Aster nodded at that, yawning, then realized how comfortable her now-healed chest was and took another long, deep breath.

"How do you feel?" Cori asked.

"Much better. Thank you."

"Good. I think you're in good shape now, but come see me downstairs if anything feels off today."

Aster nodded again. Cori's words clicked. "Wait, are you leaving? Is it morning?"

Cori gave her a sad smile. "I am; my shift starts soon. I didn't want to wake you."

"Oh."

Cori sat up part way and looked back at her. "Has anything like that ever happened before?"

Aster sighed. "No. Well, sort of. A long time ago, someone knocked my lunch out of my hand when I was walking back to my old place. But no one's ever tripped me."

"Maybe I could start coming out with you," Cori offered.

"What? Like every time? The whole time?"

"Or just to the train. I don't know. I wish I had been there."

"No," Aster said, sitting up beside her. "You don't need to do that. I'm going to use a different platform, okay? I'll take the ramp instead of the stairs. It'll be fine. That was just one asshole. Most people just give me dirty looks."

"Well, it's always an option," Cori said, touching her arm.

"No, it isn't. You need to rest before your shifts. Besides, you're my partner *and* my doctor. You can't be my bodyguard, too."

Cori pressed a kiss to her cheek and started putting her shoes on.

Aster got up to see her out, a little dizzy but otherwise feeling recovered. Cori grabbed an apple since they slept through breakfast and kissed her goodbye at the door.

Then Aster was alone in the apartment, after seeing her partner for what felt like five minutes. She sank into the sofa and rubbed her hands over her face. When she'd first moved in here, she had been so worried that she'd reflect badly on Cori, but the reality was that it was all on herself. A better option than Cori's ridiculous offer would be for Aster to move back to her old zone, but that would be a last resort—she didn't want to live separately or lose their private treatment room.

❋ ❋ ❋

The following week, Victory was more crowded than usual as travel increased ahead of Human New Year, coming up in a few days.

Heading home from another work night meant lots of

busy roads now, so Aster was sticking to side streets and alleys as much as she could after getting off at a stop farther away from their apartment as planned. She was only feeling minor discomfort in her shoulder, which was nothing that Cori couldn't heal in a few minutes, and would give them plenty of time to rest together before breakfast.

On one block, she found herself facing a group of other people. She got a bad vibe, so she doubled back to find another route, only to see a second group facing her from that direction. Turning again, she found the first group coming closer. Several of them had three blue rectangles tattooed on their necks or faces—it must mean something, but Aster had no idea what.

"Um, I don't want any trouble," she said. "I'm just on my way home."

"From where?" someone challenged.

Aster's heart was pounding in her chest. They had her completely outnumbered.

"It was, uh, a dance club over in the next zone," she tried. "Love that place."

A few people laughed and her spirits lifted, but only for a fleeting moment before the tall one in front spoke.

"A dance club, eh?" He stepped forward, cracking his knuckles in a way that might have been silly if it weren't terrifying. "Do we look like fucking gasbrains to you, whore?"

"Wait, no, please—" were the last coherent words Aster managed to say.

Alicia Haberski

✷ ✷ ✷

Cori was jolted awake by an alarm chiming on her comm—a notification that Aster Moss had been admitted to the clinic with critical injuries.

"Oh, no," she muttered, grabbing her lab coat and rushing for the door.

She had been afraid of this day, had hoped it would never come. But at least Aster made it back, and at least she did the right thing by going straight to the clinic. At least she was *alive*.

When Cori located the treatment room and stepped inside, she caught sight of Aster's pretty red hair and two nurses taking scans. All the wind was knocked from Cori's body to see her, though, because Aster had never once looked *this* bad. Her whole face was bruised and bloody, both eyes swollen shut.

"Aster," she said, coming forward and touching her shoulder. "It's me. I'm here now."

"Cori," Aster responded with a soft little sob.

"We have all her scans, and she's been given four doses of AnoDyn," said the nurse.

"Thank you," Cori said as she began to review the images.

These injuries were different than usual. They were consistent with deliberate, blunt-force trauma—the type someone might get from fists and boots . . . from other humans.

"Aster, I'm so sorry someone did this. We're going to get you fixed up. You did good, okay? You made it back here."

"Actually," a second nurse piped up, "a preacher brought her in. She said she found her like this."

"Oh," Cori said, averting her eyes for a moment and composing herself. She didn't have time to think about Aster lying on the ground, injured and alone, until a kind person came along and helped her. She didn't have time to think about her being left for dead.

At once, Cori set her focus squarely on Aster's treatment, reassuring her at every turn and calibrating the healing lamps as swiftly as possible. With the extent of the damage, it would take several hours, but thanks to the pain meds, Aster's brow had relaxed, and her breathing was even.

By the time they had treated all injuries, the swelling on Aster's face had been reduced considerably, and she was resting. Cori stayed by her side all the while, transferring her other patients to alternate doctors for the day. Now that she could allow herself to think and process, and to be alone in the room with Aster, she let her face drop to her hands and silently wept. If Cori had been with Aster, she could have protected her. She could have broken those assholes' arms before they ever touched her.

Aster stirred after some time, now able to open her eyes properly, and smacked her dry lips. Cori quickly fetched her a drink of water, which Aster took eagerly through a straw.

"There you are," Cori said, petting her hair.

"Cori," Aster said sadly, sitting up.

"Aster, don't try to mo—" Cori started, but Aster was already reaching for her.

Cori took her into a gentle hug, rubbing her back.

"I'm sorry," Aster said in a small voice. "I'm sorry."

"No, shh, it wasn't your fault. You're safe now. I've got you."

✳ ✳ ✳

When she was well enough to leave the clinic later that day, Aster could only think of one thing: a shower. Cori helped her undress in their bathroom, and moments later, Aster could finally step under the warm water. She closed her eyes and let it flow over her face, willing her mind to go blank, but in the darkness, she recalled the terror she felt when she thought she might never make it back here again.

"Aster?"

Aster opened her eyes and found Cori still standing beside the shower.

"Would you like some company?"

Aster nodded, suddenly grateful not to be alone. Cori undressed and stepped inside with her, pulling her into a gentle embrace under the hot stream. They held each other silently for a while. Aster was able to relax in the comfort of Cori's arms, feeling her heart beating against Cori's.

After some time, though, she felt the slightest heave of

Cori's shoulders. Aster didn't know what to say, so she just held her a bit tighter.

"I love you," Cori said. "I'm so glad you're okay."

"I love you, too," Aster managed. "I love you so much, Cori."

10

To the Stars

In the aftermath of the attack, Aster seemed to retreat into herself. After her shower, she was too restless to sleep, so they went to the living room. Cori stepped into the kitchen to make some tea. When she returned, she found that Aster hadn't moved an inch from where she sat down on the sofa.

"Here you go," Cori said, setting the glass on the table in front of them.

Aster just nodded, then gave her a curious look. "Are you not going back to work?"

"No, I transferred my patients for the day."

Aster's expression was blank, her sweet face still blotchy with some lingering redness and bruising.

"Listen," Cori started, hoping it wasn't too soon. "I'm not going to break my promise. I'm not going to ask you to stop doing this work. But I *am* going to ask that you stop doing it on *this* station. I think we should leave Victory now and go with your Plan B station."

Aster's eyes were glistening, a couple tears falling when she blinked. "But . . . they *need* you here."

That wasn't the response Cori had anticipated—or braced for. Her confusion must have been apparent.

"The clinic," Aster clarified. "Your other patients. How can I . . . take you away from them?"

Cori scooted closer and took her hand. "There are plenty of good doctors."

Aster shook her head, more tears falling. "Not like you. You're the best."

"Good enough, then."

Aster wiped her eyes. "I never meant to throw a wrench in your career plans."

Cori suppressed her immediate reaction to that statement, taking some time to think about what Aster must be feeling. It was technically true that when Cori had arrived on Victory nearly eight months ago, she had not imagined that she'd be leaving so soon. But she also had never imagined meeting someone like Aster.

"It's true that I might've been content to stay here longer, if we hadn't met," Cori said, rubbing Aster's back. "But I'm very glad we did. My life is only better for knowing you, for loving you and being loved by you. If that's a 'wrench' in my plans, it's a very welcome one. This place isn't safe for you anymore, and I'm not willing to be separated from you."

Aster sighed, reclining on the sofa and laying her head in Cori's lap. She was quiet for some time while Cori stroked her hair.

"Okay," she said softly. "Plan B station."

Cori squeezed her shoulder. "What *is* your Plan B station?"

"Ascension," Aster said with distaste. "There should be...a lot of options there. And a whole lot of competition. But at least I have experience now."

"Well, that settles it," Cori said with great relief. "We'll relocate as soon as possible."

✸ ✸ ✸

Nearly a week later, Cori returned home from a visit to an antiques dealer to find Aster preparing dinner. She seemed to be in better spirits now; Cori imagined that it must be because they were so close to finally leaving this awful place behind. The next ship stopping at Ascension wasn't due to depart for a few more days, which gave them plenty of time to prepare—Cori had even been able to remotely interview for a temporary opening at a clinic there, where another physician was preparing for paternal leave—but it also meant that Aster had gone longer than usual without making any payments.

"That smells wonderful," Cori said, stepping into the kitchen.

"Good," Aster replied, greeting her with an embrace. "Did you find whatever you needed at that shop?"

Cori took a moment to reply, gathering her thoughts. "Yes. In fact, I have good news. I don't want you to worry about the time between payments, so I sold a few things that will cover the next one for you."

Aster blinked, brow furrowed. "What did you—?" Her gaze darted to the empty corner shelf. "Oh...no. Not your *books*. Right?"

"They would have been cumbersome to lug around, anyway. It'll be fun to start a new collection, really."

"I wouldn't have wanted you to—"

"I know. That's why I didn't mention it before. I want you to have a real break for now. You don't owe me anything. Not even gratitude. Just please let me pay one for you."

Aster looked at her with damp eyes and pulled her into a tight hug, which Cori returned.

✳ ✳ ✳

With time to spare before they left Victory for good, Cori had one final connection she hoped to make on the station. To do so, she paid a visit to a place she had never been: the small interfaith temple in their zone.

Inside were neat rows of empty benches, tattered with age, and a pleasant, spicy scent permeating the room. She was distracted for a moment by a person on their way out, who stopped to draw a circle over their heart with one finger—Cori recalled seeing the same gesture a few times on Idun.

"May I be of help to you?" asked a preacher in a gray robe.

"Yes," Cori said. "I'm looking for a member of your clergy. Someone who helped an injured woman to the clinic last week?"

"That was me," came a voice to her left. "Is she alright?"

Cori turned to find a woman her own height in a matching gray robe, her dark hair swept into a neat bun.

"She did, thanks to your help," Cori said, chest heavy with emotion. "I wanted to personally thank you, preacher— Sorry, I don't know how to properly address you."

"Miranda will do," she said with a kind smile. "But your thanks isn't necessary. I'm glad to know she's well."

"It's necessary for me. She's my partner. I may not be a Believer myself, but I will be deeply grateful to you for the rest of my life. I wanted to be sure to tell you that before we leave the station."

"Doctor..." Miranda started.

"Cori, please."

"Cori," she repeated, smile falling. "Of course. She was asking for you when I found her. *I'm* thankful, too, that I was in the right place at the right time and given the opportunity to help her. You say you're traveling soon?"

"Yes, we're moving to a new station."

"Then I'll pray for a safe journey."

"I appreciate that," Cori said. "And... Miranda?"

"Yes?"

"Could I embrace you?"

She smiled at that. "Of course."

After leaving the temple, Cori decided not to mention the visit to Aster, at least for now. She worried that the whole experience was still too raw, and she didn't want to force her to relive it in any way.

✻ ✻ ✻

Departing their apartment for the last time, Aster felt numb to all of it. It was odd to walk away from the one place on Victory she might actually miss. And it was hard to feel great about going to fucking Ascension Station, where the future was so uncertain.

"You alright?" Cori asked, carrying both of their suitcases into the elevator, plus her own backpack.

"Yeah. You sure you don't need any help with those?"

"What? Oh, gosh, no. It's nothing."

Aster nodded, feeling kind of useless.

In the train on the way to the station's transit port, Aster leaned into Cori and felt her press a kiss to her hair.

"Almost there. You'll never have to come back here."

Aster took her hand. "It wasn't all bad."

Cori laced their fingers together. "No, it wasn't."

They rode in silence after that. Aster let herself picture the two of them living happily together sometime in the future, when her debts were repaid and she was free. She could take Cori to her home station and introduce her to her mothers. The thought made her chest a little tight; she'd never gone this long without visiting home before. The last time she'd seen her family was well before the smuggling-job-turned-disaster. Her moms could never know what was really going on, so she'd just written that she had a job on a parcel delivery ship with a busy route and would have a full schedule for the near future. She hadn't told them *anything* about life on Victory.

After leaving the train and boarding the transport ship, they found their private cabin and settled in. Aster went into the small ensuite bathroom while Cori put their bags away. In the mirror, Aster looked tired and anxious, but at least fully healed.

Back in the main room of their cabin, Aster came up behind Cori and embraced her.

"Hi," Cori said, turning around and kissing her.

"Cori . . ." Aster said, unable to keep her voice from wavering.

"What is it?"

"Cori," Aster repeated. "I'm not willing to be separated from *you*, either . . . I hope you know that. I'm imagining rosy futures for us now."

"Good," Cori said with a smile.

"You've done so much for me," Aster went on, "and we'll have a happy, cozy, boring life someday. I promise."

There came the faint shift of the ship entering hyperspace, with the familiar sensation of a static charge that jolted Aster's organs. Cori reacted with a little flinch.

"You alright?" Aster asked.

Cori took a breath and met her gaze. "I love you. I want that future for us, too. But I don't need you to promise me anything. Being with you . . . it's already more happiness than I ever imagined for myself. No matter what happens, I'll always be grateful for that. I'll always be grateful just to know you."

Aster seized her, pulling Cori to her lips and kissing her with vigor. There was no way words would ever be enough. Cori matched her eagerness, and they fell into bed shortly after, pulling off each other's clothes in a flurry.

After they had undressed, Cori was swiftly above her and trailing kisses across her body, from her mouth to her navel and then lower still. Aster basked in it, dizzy with desire after going so long without her touch. Cori seemed to feel the same urgency, moving up to kiss her lips and rocking her thigh against her. That position would normally take a while to send Aster over the edge . . . but this time it happened in minutes.

Aster switched with her, then, pushing her to the mattress and getting on top to return the favor. She wasn't positive, but she thought Cori looked turned on *and* amused by the assertiveness. She was so, so beautiful, eyes fluttering shut and full lips parted as her chest heaved. They carried on for a while, enjoying each other in all the ways they'd both missed. By the time they were spent, Aster had lost track of time. All she could do was pant and laugh a little, as Cori pressed lazy kisses to her arm and shoulder.

They drifted to sleep sometime later, resting in each other's arms in the dim cabin, as the ship carried them toward their new home.

11
Ascension

The one time Aster had been to Ascension Station when she was younger, she had found it overwhelming and pretentious. In the years since then, the station had apparently attempted to redefine those words.

Making their way to their new residence meant being bombarded with walls of glowing screens, twinkling lights, and hovercab traffic overhead, amongst crowds of people in all sorts of absurdly colorful party attire. Aster fought an urge to roll her eyes, trying to stay vaguely positive, since she was the reason they were here.

Cori, on the other hand, beamed as she watched a large robotic butterfly pass overhead. "This is incredible!" She weaved through the crowd to the railing overlooking the hub's main courtyard. Aster followed. From there, they had a full view of the massive celebration below, with dancers and floats and people enjoying booze and treats and live music, which was an average night on Ascension. Aster was glad to have missed the Human New Year celebrations here, at least. "I had no idea places like this existed," Cori said with a happy laugh.

It gets old fast, Aster wanted to say. It did have its novelty, but she couldn't look at it with the same wonder. It was all so loud and chaotic and frivolous.

Ascension was divided into six hubs, or three double-hubs split down the center by a massive multilevel highway for efficient cross-station transportation. Their new "condo" was above the station's main medical center, located in the central double-hub. The space couldn't have been more in contrast to where they'd lived on Victory—this one had teal walls, furniture with gold accents, a wall screen that took up an *entire* living room wall, plus smaller screens in the bedrooms and shower. Thanks to the request Cori put through, the second bedroom was already set up for private treatment.

They also had a decent view of a side street, which Aster was quietly happy about. She couldn't imagine looking down on a wild party all the time.

"Well," Cori said, dropping onto the enormous white sofa. "This is home for a while."

Aster took that as her cue to sit on her lap. "At least it's cozy."

They kissed. Aster felt Cori's hands remove her hair tie so that her waves fell loose around her shoulders and Cori could run her fingers gently through the locks. Aster relaxed into her, melting at her touch. When she shut out everything else and just sat there with her partner, it did feel like an okay place to call home. She hoped she could hang onto that feeling.

✳ ✳ ✳

The following day, after sleeping late in their ridiculously plush bed, Aster set out to explore. Ascension was somewhat more tolerable, and less neon, in the daylight cycle, with tourists mostly out for shopping or sight-seeing, and a respite from the massive party vibe.

Her first stop was a tech shop, where she made the reluctant but practical purchase of a pair of interface contacts. She had used similar contacts on a few other interface-enabled stations, but Ascension was known for offering a very smooth and pleasant interface experience. (Because of course it was.)

With each delicate contact placed in her eyes moments later, she was prompted to create her user profile and then shown a "menu" of interests to check so that the station could display relevant info as she walked around. She bypassed that for now and set out, noting the way the interface offered glimmering bubbles next to each store and sign and pathway, which she could point or double blink at if she wanted details. Larger bubbles—oddly pretty, without being distracting—hovered next to other interface users, offering public profile info, which was usually just their name and gender and whether or not they were open for private messages. She left her channel closed for now, since she wasn't in the mood to be bombarded with ads and coupons, nor did she want to pay to block them.

She wandered the avenues of bars and nightclubs to get acquainted with the layout. It was even more glitzy and excessive than she remembered. Visiting a popular block meant walking under sparkling archways and flying robotic animals, all below a simulated blue sky. On a single street, she passed dozens of colorful building facades offering food or shopping or drinks or sim cafes or gas bars or luxury lounges or strip clubs or casinos—or, in some cases, all of the above. Each one tried to look unique, and the combined result was a truly dizzying array of options and visuals. But that was the draw of this place, for so many.

Passing by a group of people wearing matching shirts and *screaming* with excitement as they approached a popular lunch place, she shook her head—it was one thing to have resorted to a party station, but it pained her to think that she dragged *Cori* into this place.

After a while, she moved on from her sight-seeing errand and used the interface to search for a grocery store. The route arrows that rendered on the ground seconds later were pretty handy, she had to admit.

Back in the condo, as she started making dinner, she

tried and failed not to worry about the impending evening. The only thing worse than the idea that Ascension would have plenty of options was the possibility that it might *not*.

Cori threw her arms around her when she returned from her shift.

"How was your first day?" Aster asked.

"It went well! Everyone seems really nice. Lots of introductions and forms and policies and not many patients, but that's normal."

"Right. The boring part."

"Exactly. How was yours?"

"Fine," she said with a shrug. "Dinner's almost ready."

Cori gave her a look with a hint of sympathy. "Nervous?"

"Yeah. But I skipped lunch, so mostly just starving."

As they ate, Cori eased the tension by talking about the doctors she met and the updated equipment at the clinic. Aster was grateful for the distraction and glad that she only needed to nod along. All the while, though, anxiety washed through her chest and pooled in her gut. What if there was *too much* competition? What if clients here weren't willing to pay her usual rates? What if she wasn't cut out for this work outside of a shithole where she was rare as a unicorn?

After dinner, when she was dressed and made up, she took a long breath and tried to clear her head. Seemingly reading her mind, Cori took hold of her shoulders and gave her a pointed look.

"You'll be alright," she said. "Maybe it's different here,

but you'll get the hang of it. Don't put too much pressure on yourself. And ... be careful, please."

Aster nodded. "Always."

When she made it down to the ground level, Cori sent her a string of hearts through the interface, and Aster smiled. She sent one back, glad to be connected in that way—they'd given each other direct message permissions. Cori didn't need any contacts, since she had fancy military tech in her head that allowed her to connect to the interface with no exterior devices.

Once she was out and walking, Aster felt an odd sense of relief. The moment she had been dreading was finally here, and she could get this first night over with.

The same avenues she explored during the day were barely recognizable in the dim lighting of the night cycle, with bright screens and holograms and people handing out freebies and beads and other incentives to passers-by. The sky simulation had changed not to a typical nighttime starscape, but an ever-shifting nebula that gave the streets a colorful glow. Her attire didn't stand out *at all* in this place, and she was trying to figure out how to brand herself as available when a large ad display caught her eye—it was promoting something called "personal listings" with a shimmering bubble. After blinking at the bubble, her jaw dropped: There was an entire *network* of listings of sex workers for hire, organized by those in closest proximity to her location. Lots of their ads looked professionally shot and showed them waving and posing as she scanned through.

"Hey baby," one of them said, apparently having enabled audio. "New in town? Let me help you *ascend*. Tap me *right here* for a first time disc—"

Irritated, she waved her hand to close that page. How the fuck could she compete with all that? The idea of paying for a frilly photoshoot and listing cutesy little ads to appeal to wealthy strangers was revolting. Her heart sank at the thought that she might be totally out of her depth.

As she continued on, something else dawned on her: For the most part, there were only humans on these blocks, even in the evening. Based on what she remembered about Ascension, she had expected more of a species mix, but she had only seen a couple aliens so far. Maybe she just needed to find *those* zones and the competition wouldn't be so steep. Maybe.

Riding a train to try to get out of the human-dominant area, she got off a few zones over, significantly removed from the central hub, and immediately spotted a few Orykters nearby—that was a good sign. Turning down a new avenue, she caught sight of an Irsid having a private chat with a human and stopped in her tracks, thinking they might be initiating a transaction, but then the pair sat on a bench to gas up together.

Pausing at a corner in front of an odd building with dramatic columns and dark windows, Aster accessed the station map to get her bearings. She knew she couldn't give up yet. If there was anywhere in the galaxy where individuals of all species were dying to spend money on ridiculous shit, it was Ascension. She just had to find the right ones.

After a few minutes, she felt a tap on her shoulder and turned to find a tall reptilian alien looking down at her—an Umblyrhyn, with dark green scales covering their unclothed body. Aster hadn't worked with any of them before; there weren't many on Victory, and the ones that did show up never seemed interested in her. This one grunted something at her that she couldn't understand. It took her a second to realize she had a pop-up in her feed with an option to translate.

Price for three hours?

It took Aster a moment to believe it—was that really the first question out of their mouth? Trying her luck, she responded with her typical rate, bracing for the lizard to haggle.

Instead, they retrieved their comm from the satchel at their hip without hesitation. The payment, in full all at once, was confirmed on her feed moments later.

"Wow," Aster said out loud. "Well, I'm all yours now—"

The lizard held out a collar with a chain leash, waiting.

"Oh, okay," she said, reluctantly buckling the collar around her neck. "This is new."

Just as it clicked into place, auto-adjusting to the size of her neck, the lizard was leading her forward, up the wide steps toward the strange, dark building. Aster scrambled to keep up. She couldn't imagine what they would be doing in a public place, but with the amount of money she just made, she wasn't about to protest.

As it turned out, nothing could have prepared her for what she saw upon stepping through the door. She was standing in what looked like an Umblyrhyn nightclub, extremely warm and balmy, with lounge pools and flat furniture throughout. All around them were other lizards enjoying drinks and happily grunting or even dancing to low, distorted "music" that sounded to Aster's human ears like something out of a nightmare.

Then things got *weird*.

As her client greeted some acquaintances and they turned and noticed her, their expressions shifted. They looked...excited. One of them approached her, cooing, and started petting her head, running their claws gently through her hair. When they jutted out their tongue and touched her cheek, though, the client tugged her chain and swatted them away. The other lizard made a sound not unlike laughing and returned to their seat. Aster's client continued deeper into the club. As they went, other lizards reached out to pet her. She wasn't certain, but it seemed like her client was walking with a proud posture; this showing off must be part of what they paid so much for. So, not too bad so far.

That's when she noticed the cages. They had reached the center of the room, where a former dance floor was covered with several rows of shiny cages, each with just enough room for a human to kneel—as evidenced by the other leashed people inside. Aster considered bolting now, giving the client a refund and running out of this place and never returning, but she made eye-contact with one of the caged people, which auto-opened a profile box. It was a young woman named Joely with long blue hair and glowing irises. She gave Aster two thumbs up, smiling wide. Looking more closely at the others, Aster realized that none appeared to be in any distress, so maybe this would be fine. Aster ducked down to enter an empty cage at the end of a row, dropping to her knees on the cushion inside and hoping it wouldn't be a choice she regretted. The client hooked her chain to the top, petted her head, and shut the little cage door.

Looking around and trying not to panic, she found the cage next to hers occupied by a man named Patrek, wearing thick eyeliner and a mesh top. He gave her a quick wink and turned his attention to a lizard who had walked up with a drink. At the sight of it, Patrek started licking his lips and nodding, and the lizard poured it through the bars *directly onto his face*, soaking his hair while he held his mouth open. Aster was slack-jawed as she witnessed this, wondering if maybe she had been drugged at some point in the evening and this was all just an intense hallucination.

A moment later, Aster's client walked up to her cage with a similar drink. She looked back at the guy next to her, who nodded in urgent encouragement. Aster definitely didn't want to make the client angry, so she played along, feigning thirst and holding her mouth open as the liquid rushed down. It had a pleasant, fruity taste.

Some time passed in that way, with lizards standing around watching while others bought drinks for the caged humans who would eagerly lap them up. After a while, one lizard walked over to a cage and let a human out—the short woman with blue hair, who jumped up and clapped. Her client took hold of her leash, and they disappeared into an adjoining room.

Aster's nerves returned in full force as she wondered what that meant, but Patrek only looked bored. He caught her gaze and gave her a thumbs-up, raising his eyebrows in question. Aster returned the gesture and nodded, though she didn't feel *good* about any of this.

Her client reappeared shortly to open her cage and remove her, leash first, and then Aster was led to the mysterious other room. It turned out to be an area with private booths. Her client located an empty one, entered, and shut the door behind them. The walls of the small room muted the music a bit, which was a nice change for Aster's ears. The lizard took out their comm again, and Aster got a swift notification that they had submitted a new payment of about ten percent of the first.

"Wow," Aster said again, because she couldn't think of anything else.

The lizard grunted. *Happy*, the translation said, and they

reached out two fingers to gently poke at the corners of her mouth.

"Oh, yes," Aster agreed, forcing an awkward smile. "Very happy!"

With that, the client moved to pet her all over with their smooth, scaly hands, taking care not to touch her with the claws. Next, they began to remove her clothing. They were apparently experienced with that, having no trouble with the zippers and setting everything neatly aside. Once she was undressed, they returned to touching her . . . and then the *licking* started. The fruity drink had drenched her face and dripped down her torso, and now it seemed the client was "cleaning" it from her skin.

When Aster emerged from the booth sometime later, clothed and unleashed and absolutely coated in lizard saliva, the crowd had thinned. She made her way quickly out the door and down the steps. Back on the street and once again in reality, she pulled up her account to confirm she wasn't imagining any of those payments and saw the largest number she had ever managed in a single night.

All she could do was laugh.

"Hey," came a voice beside her. It was Patrek, the man who had been next to her in the cages. He was shorter than her—most likely a grounder—and his brunette curls were just as slick with saliva as her own hair felt.

"Hey," she said back, glad to be able to hear him. "Thanks for the emotional support."

He nodded. "First time?"

"I'm sure that was obvious."

"I saw the fear in your eyes," he said, grinning.

Before their conversation could continue, they were surrounded by a group of cheering people—the others from the cages.

Patrek smiled and shook his head. "They're a rowdy bunch, but they're fun."

"I got *goodies,*" Joely—the woman with blue hair from before—said, holding up a packet of orange pills.

The others, except for Patrek, reacted with excitement and held out their hands.

"We're going to Zion, right?" one person asked.

"Yeahhhh!" Joely yelled with a pill on her tongue.

"What's Zion?" Aster asked no one in particular.

"Only the *best* human club on Ascension," said a curvy, bald woman, leaning on Joely's shoulder as she took her own pill with flourish. "You in?"

Aster realized, belatedly, that she was also being offered a pill.

"Oh, no thanks," she said, declining both offers at once. "Maybe next time."

"It was her first time here, guys," Patrek said. "It's a lot to process."

"Oh my STARS I'm so JEALOUS," Joely said. "That first time is such a *wild* ride."

"Wild is a good word," Aster agreed, and the others laughed.

With that, they started in separate directions, and Patrek waved goodbye. "See you around."

※ ※ ※

As she rode a train in a daze, Aster realized she probably should have asked for more information from those people about the work they did. She could have asked Patrek for tips of the trade, but her head was spinning too much to think of that before.

Back at the condo, Cori greeted her at the door.

"Hi!" she said, reaching out for her before Aster could warn her not to.

"Hi. I'm fine; I just need a shower."

"Yes . . . you do," Cori said, looking curiously at the goo on her hand. "I take it you had some success?"

"I did . . . You know, I don't normally tell you about it, but I think this time I *have* to."

"Oh? Okay!"

After Aster was finally, blessedly clean and wrapped in a fluffy robe, they sat on the sofa together and she gave Cori a play-by-play of the bizarre outing. She enjoyed the way Cori laughed with her at the absurdities—it was actually fun to share a work night with her in such detail.

"Well, this station is full of surprises," Cori remarked. "Do you think you'll go back again?"

"I'm trying to decide," Aster admitted. "It was pretty fucking weird, but the pay was good, and I guess it's not too dangerous if they have regulars?"

Cori nodded.

"What do *you* think?" Aster asked.

"I think it's completely up to you. If you're not too uncomfortable, you could try it a couple more times just to see if it'll work?"

"Yeah, that's true."

Cori leaned over to press a kiss to her cheek. "I'm glad your first night out was decent."

Aster moved to kiss her properly in reply.

"Did you *want* to go with the others afterward? To that club?" Cori asked.

"Oh, I don't know. They were the raver type; they'll probably be out all night. And I knew you'd be waiting for me."

Cori smiled. "Well, don't be afraid to have some fun out there, okay? It doesn't have to be all business."

Aster kissed her again. "Speaking of *fun*: Now that I have my first job figured out, we can go do some exploring? Maybe have a nice dinner?"

"Yes! I'd love that."

12

Little Eden

For their first dinner date on Ascension, Aster left the choice of restaurant up to Cori. Wholly overwhelmed by the selection in the guides, Cori asked a colleague one day in passing —Dr. Kiran Alvarez, a friendly neurologist who had lived on the station for some time.

"Well, what kinds of food do you like?" Kiran asked with their signature charm.

"Gosh, I'll try anything... That doesn't help, though."

Kiran chuckled. "Okay. What kind of *atmosphere* are you looking for?"

Cori thought that over for a moment. "Well, there was this neat restaurant on Victory that was decorated to look like a nature scene on a planet. I liked that!"

"Hmm. Okay. Important question: Are you alright with it being *ultra* romantic?"

"Absolutely!"

"Boom," Kiran said, grinning. "I know the perfect place."

That evening, dressing for dinner, Cori felt like she was radiating excitement. It was so wonderful to be going out on their new home station, especially since Aster would be able to relax and enjoy herself without worrying about work options.

"You look beautiful," Cori said as Aster emerged in her maroon top and dark pants, paired with shiny black heels. Her hair was side-swept to show off a sparkly ear cuff, and her eyes were lined with dark makeup. It was an outfit Cori had seen a couple times, and it never failed to make her weak at the knees.

"Thanks," Aster said with a little laugh. "You look *gorgeous*. I've never seen this before!"

An odd heat rushed to Cori's face. She couldn't claim to understand fashion, typically opting for comfort over style, but she was fond of her current ensemble: A soft black top with thin straps that left her shoulders bare, paired with a floor-length silver skirt that reminded her of a sparkly fish tail.

"Thank you," she said. "It's been a while since I've worn it, but this feels like the right place."

Catching a train just outside their apartment, they were whisked toward the restaurant. Among the other travelers, their clothes didn't stand out, but Cori hardly noticed the rest of them anyway, since she couldn't seem to stop looking at Aster—who caught her staring and smiled, taking her hand.

Despite the station's size and the restaurant being in the next hub over, they arrived in under ten minutes thanks to the efficient transportation system.

Not wanting to spoil the surprise, Cori had taken Kiran's recommendation at their word and simply made a reservation at a restaurant called Little Eden. But even if she *had* peeked at photos, nothing could have prepared her for the splendor of stepping through the door.

"Oh, wow," she said under her breath.

"Holy shit," Aster echoed.

The place looked like an enchanted garden from a fantasy film—or perhaps a dream. Every table Cori could see was nestled in its own round booth, hugged by what looked like *wooden* trees with winding branches bearing pink blossoms and glowing lanterns to provide ambient table lighting. Above them, a strikingly pretty sky simulation obscured the ceiling, with an impossible amount of sparkling stars that shifted and shimmered as patches of puffy gray clouds rolled over, glowing with starlight.

As a host led them to their table, Cori had Aster's hand in a firm grasp, partly in excitement and partly to maintain her anchor to reality. The restaurant, if it could even be referred to by such a simple term, only grew more extravagant as they walked deeper inside: There was a stream running through the center of the floor that flowed over a drop-off and became a cascading waterfall, bordered by more tree booths stair-stepped down a mossy hill, leading to a picturesque lake at the base. Above, in the sky, Cori's eyes were drawn to the brightest spot—a moon, spilling ethereal white light into the clouds around it. Around them, in the air, little floating lights twinkled and vanished at random intervals. Cori couldn't seem to catch sight of one long enough to tell what they were.

Their table was near the lake, giving them a nice view of the hill and waterfall. When they stepped into the booth, the flowering tree branches and lanterns looked even prettier up close. Cori could see now that Kiran's description of the place as "ultra romantic" was actually an understatement.

When she finally tore her eyes away from the scenery and looked at Aster, she found her happy and rosy-cheeked.

"Ah-ha!" Cori said, triumphant. "I *knew* we'd find a place on the station you actually liked."

Aster laughed. "It's beautiful. I do feel underdressed, though."

"Well, your date thinks you look perfect."

"That's all that matters to me," Aster said sweetly, leaning in for a kiss.

Maybe it was the incredible atmosphere, or the semi-privacy of the booth, but something came over Cori and she couldn't seem to stop kissing Aster for a while. That is, until a server appeared and took their drink orders.

In the space that followed, Cori looked at Aster, and they laughed together.

"I'm really glad we're here," Aster said, and Cori knew she wasn't just talking about the restaurant.

"Me, too."

A chorus of cheers erupted nearby. When the server returned with their drinks, Cori couldn't help but be curious. "Is there a celebration?"

The server took a moment to parse her meaning. "Oh, yes! There's a newly engaged trio over there. Very happy night for them."

"Oh, that's lovely," Cori remarked.

"That must happen pretty often here," Aster observed.

"Several times per week," the server said with a smile.

They sat in silence as they reviewed the lengthy menu via the interface. By the time they gave the server their meal orders, Cori had sort of forgotten that previous conversation, so she was confused when Aster suddenly asked, "Is that something *you* want?"

"Is what? Dessert?"

"No," Aster said with a laugh. "Marriage."

"Oh," she said. "It's a nice thought, but not something I'd ever insist on."

Aster smiled. "I know you wouldn't. I'm just asking if you *want* it. Someday."

"Someday," Cori repeated, taking a sip of her drink. "Honestly, I have given it some thought since we've been together, and I like the idea... But all I really *want* in the future is to be with you. Anything more, *someday*, is a bonus."

Aster nodded at that. Cori hoped it was a good answer.

"Do *you* want it?" Cori asked.

Aster met her gaze, eyes sparkling in the lantern light, and then nodded again. "I never have before. Never wanted that with anyone, never really thought that far ahead. So it feels strange to admit it, but yes. With you? It's a very nice thought."

Abruptly, Cori's heart was pounding, because she knew she needed to confess something she *probably* should have said a long time ago. "It's new for me, too."

"Really?" Aster asked with a smile.

"Very new, yes," Cori said, feeling overly warm. "But... you're the first person I've ever dated."

Aster blinked, her smile falling. "Wait, first? First *ever*?"

Their first course arrived and sat untouched before them.

"To be fair, I never sought it out," Cori said, scrambling to rescue the moment. "While I lived on Idun, I buried myself in my courses and my research and my books, and that felt like enough—like a dream life, really—but I also never met *anyone* who made me *want* anything like that, and after a while I assumed I never would, and, oh... gosh, I'm rambling."

"Cori," Aster said, looking understandably stunned.

"I'm sorry. I didn't mean to spoil the moment."

"When we... that was the first time you'd *ever*—"

Cori nodded. "Yes. Regardless of how you fill in the blank, yes."

Aster looked the tiniest bit sad. "Why didn't you tell me?"

"I just didn't want you to feel any pressure," Cori admitted. "I was afraid you'd feel like you had to . . . *educate* me. I wanted everything to be comfortable."

Brow still furrowed, Aster reached out to take her hand. "It wouldn't have been uncomfortable at all."

Cori squeezed her hand. "I know. I should have told you much sooner."

"I hope I never pushed you into—" Aster started, and Cori quickly shook her head.

"No. Never. You were *wonderful*."

"I guess I shouldn't have assumed anything . . . It does make sense in retrospect." Aster started to laugh. "I thought you just *really* liked kissing."

Cori laughed with her. "Oh, I do! As I've discovered!"

Aster dissolved into more laughter, dropping her head into her hands.

After they belatedly enjoyed their first course, Aster scooted closer in the booth and slid her arm around Cori's waist.

"Love you," Aster said softly.

"I love you, too," Cori replied. They kissed again.

In the silence that followed, Cori found that some lingering guilt had pooled inside her.

"Aster?"

"Hmm?"

"I'm sorry if I hurt you. By withholding that."

"No. Hey, look at me. I'm sorry you were ever afraid to tell me. It wouldn't have changed anything; I just would have understood you better." Aster pressed a kiss to Cori's cheek. "Listen, when this is all over—when I'm free and I can put this kind of work behind me, I'm going to ask you a really important question, okay?"

Cori felt a rush of emotion, too strong to contain. "Okay."

She pulled Aster into a tight hug. They held each other for a while under their pretty little tree. For a moment, everything else evaporated, and it was just the two of them, floating in a perfect garden in their own corner of the universe.

When they came back to reality, Aster took a napkin and dabbed Cori's cheeks. They continued their meal. Each course was uniquely delicious, and by the time their desserts arrived, they were talking and laughing and reacting with awe at the decadent treats.

✳ ✳ ✳

On the train back to their apartment, their arms were perpetually entwined. Aster couldn't seem to stop looking at Cori, knowing what she now knew. In hindsight, so many things made more sense—particularly how shocked Cori had been when Aster had admitted that she returned her feelings. She felt silly for never putting it together, but in fairness to herself, the idea of someone as attractive and friendly as Cori never dating anyone throughout college and medical school just hadn't dawned on her. She had been so smooth and confident when she told Aster how she felt, plus she'd offered *oral* the first time they were intimate. With sudden clarity, Aster realized Cori must have done thorough research on sex beforehand.

Aster abruptly broke the silence with laughter and cupped her mouth.

"What is it?" Cori asked with a smile.

"It's nothing. Just thinking." Aster kissed her cheek and then leaned into her for the rest of the ride.

Back in the privacy of their home, Aster didn't hesitate to sweep Cori into her arms. She remembered all the times Cori had approached their intimacy with so much caution and care, repeatedly checking to be sure Aster was alright. She might have done the same if she had known that Cori was new to all of it.

They ended up on the sofa, with Aster straddling Cori's lap, kissing her and thinking about the first time they kissed, also on a sofa back on Victory. And their first-ever dinner they'd shared not long before that, when Cori had been brave enough to speak her mind.

Aster paused, leaning back just enough to look at her and touch her face. "Thank you."

"For what?" Cori asked.

"For *this*. You made this happen. We're together because of you. I never could have been the one who spoke up first... I didn't have your courage."

Cori pulled her into a new kiss. "I can hardly take all the credit. When *you* had the courage to give me a chance."

They resumed their affection, grasping at the fabric of each other's tops, when Aster had an idea. She leaned back again, looking at Cori with a smile this time. "Let me start," she said, reaching for the sides of Cori's shirt and pulling it slowly upward while holding eye contact.

A hint of color rose to Cori's cheeks, and Aster inwardly celebrated. She wanted to make sure the pretty restaurant wasn't the only reason this was a night to remember. With the shirt off, she dipped to press her lips to Cori's chest, trailing light kisses across her breasts and collarbones in the same way Cori had often done for her.

Next, she kissed Cori's lips once more, then stood to undress herself.

Cori started to follow, but Aster put out her hand.

"Wait. Just... stay there for a minute."

Cori gave her a curious look, resettling into the sofa. Aster unbuttoned and removed her own shirt, and then her pants, hoping she looked seductive rather than ridiculous.

When she was down to her bra and panties, she sank to her knees and leaned forward, running her fingers up Cori's legs as she lifted the hem of her skirt and planted a kiss on her inner thigh. She heard a small gasp in reply.

"Oh," Cori said, apparently catching up.

"Is this alright?"

Cori gave her a quick nod, but her wide-eyed stare seemed anxious. Aster raised up off the floor to lean forward and kiss her again.

"You sure?" she asked.

"Definitely," Cori said with happy enthusiasm. "Please continue."

"Good," Aster said, pecking her mouth again. "You're stunning like this."

"So are you," Cori said in a breathless whisper.

Encouraged, Aster returned to her lap, pushing the skirt up with haste and moving her underwear aside.

She gave Cori a little smirk and then went to work with her mouth, moving her tongue slowly to start. Cori hummed in response, taking a firm grasp of her shoulder. Encouraged, Aster increased her speed and pressure, bracing herself between Cori's legs.

With the sounds Cori was making, Aster could tell that it probably wouldn't take long, so she paced herself, pausing to use her hand for a moment before resuming. All the while, Cori's grasp on her shoulder held steady.

"Do you want to stay here," Aster asked after a while, "or get in bed?"

Cori looked at her with hazy eyes—and flushed cheeks.

"*Completely* up to you," Aster added quickly, before Cori could deflect the question.

"Oh," Cori said with a little smile, "well, in that case . . . maybe I could just . . . take this off."

Aster smiled back, bracing herself on Cori's knee as she stood. "Alright. Come here."

She helped Cori off the sofa and kissed her, and then Cori stepped out of her remaining clothes and set them aside. They were kissing again immediately, nude bodies pressed together. Aster relished the feeling of Cori's warmth against her.

Reclining on the wide sofa this time, Aster fell back into place and finished what she started, bringing Cori to a peak that had her legs shaking as a moan dissolved into laughter.

In the moment that followed, Cori swiftly sat up again, pulling Aster to her lips. Straddling her lap, Aster felt her hand a second later—it was her turn to gasp.

"Oh, you're so—" Cori breathed. "May I?"

Aster nodded, eyes clamping shut in the next moment as Cori touched her in exactly the way she liked. She was already so aroused that two fingers slipped in easily, while Cori's thumb steadily rubbed her clit.

"Ah, fuck," she said, letting her head loll back.

Cori kissed her neck. "You're amazing."

When Aster came, she cried out and arched her back. Cori's strong arm anchored her in place, while the other hand kept a steady pace until Aster collapsed against her.

WHERE STARLIGHT BURNS

They stayed on the sofa for a while, panting, before they gained the energy to get up and shower together.

That night, as she fell asleep, Aster looked at Cori's peaceful form lying beside her and smiled. A bumpy road may have led her to this moment, and there would certainly be more challenges ahead, but tonight, she was happy—and exactly where she wanted to be.

✺ ✺ ✺

Aster slept late the next day and wandered into the kitchen around lunch time, still basking in the glow of their nice date.

Her comm buzzed—she didn't have her contacts in—and she found that Cori had messaged her a string of hearts. With a little laugh, Aster responded in kind, with her own string of hearts in another color.

A moment later, her comm buzzed again.

Are you home?

Aster blinked, now twice surprised. *Yes?*

I have lunch free if you'll be in for a while?

Come on! :)

A few minutes later, Aster heard the door open and called out from the kitchen. "Want me to make sandwiches or som—"

She was cut off by Cori pulling her into her arms and kissing her as though they hadn't seen each other in weeks.

"Hi," Cori said.

"Hi?" Aster said, still surprised.

"I can't stop thinking about you. About last night."

Aster smiled. "Me, too. It was a good night."

"It was better than *good*," Cori said, cheeks rosy. "It was amazing."

"I take it we'll be returning."

"Returning?" Cori asked, suddenly confused. "We're here already."

"Wait," Aster said, now equally confused. "What *part* of last night are we talking about?"

"Are you joking?!"

"I'm not . . . I mean, it was a really nice date?"

Cori gave her a look of exaggerated frustration. "The whole evening was very nice, yes, but I am *talking about* the part that happened *here*. When you did a kind of . . . spontaneous striptease?"

"Oh," Aster said in surprise. "I'm glad you liked it."

"Liked it?" Cori asked in the same incredulous tone. "I've never been so . . . um."

Aster laughed, suddenly noticing how red Cori's face was. "Come here."

With limited time on Cori's lunch break, they moved swiftly to the bedroom, where they undressed rapidly and fell into bed, using their hands on each other at the same time—almost like they were racing. Aster found it fun to be intimate with such haste, enjoying the thought that Cori had rushed up to their condo *specifically* for this.

Afterward, Cori took Aster's face in her hands and kissed her once more, for several seconds, before she let go and reluctantly stood to get dressed. Aster just lay there watching her. When Cori turned back, she gave Aster a look.

"You're making it pretty hard to leave. Lying there looking like that."

"Sorry." Aster laughed and stood to embrace her. "I'm glad you had a break."

Cori hummed a little laugh. "Me, too."

Another long kiss followed.

After Cori was gone again and Aster remembered to eat something, she realized that this was the most she'd ever felt like she and Cori were an average couple. This is what their lives could be like, one day, when they could live wherever they wanted, and their greatest concern was wishing for longer lunch breaks. That was a lovely thought.

13

Zion

On Aster's second work night on Ascension, she arrived at the lizard club earlier in the evening and found other people for hire—including a few she recognized—standing in a line out front, at the base of the steps.

It took her a moment to spot Patrek, since he had dyed his hair bright red.

"Hello again," she said, stepping up beside him.

"Hi," he said with a smile. "Didn't know if you'd be back."

"First time wasn't so bad." She shrugged.

He laughed. "The weirdness wears off pretty fast, honestly."

An Umblyrhyn emerged from the club and regarded the group from afar, prompting a few people to wave and offer coy hellos. The lizard stepped up to a short woman with green hair in long pigtails, whom Aster belatedly recognized as Joely. As the lizard secured her collar, she jumped up and down, clapping.

"She knows how to put on a show," Aster remarked.

Patrek just smiled. "Hey, listen."

Aster met his gaze.

"Just so you know, if you want to be a regular here, you should change up your look—hair color maybe, and different types of outfits. They don't usually recognize our faces, but they'll remember the more obvious details. They want to see something new."

"Good advice," Aster said. "Thanks. Anything else I should know?"

"Just... try not to look bored or scared. They'll tip better if you seem like you're having a good time."

"Interesting."

A lizard approached Patrek, and he snapped his attention to them, gasping in faux surprise. As he was led away by the leash, he gave Aster a wink.

"See you in there."

Aster took it as a good sign that he seemed so certain she'd be chosen, and sure enough, a lizard eventually approached her and quickly submitted payment—nearly four times the amount Aster would've made from one client back on Victory.

So *that* made it pretty easy to act happy as she was leashed up.

What followed was essentially the same as before, with

her client—this one shorter and greener than the one before—leading her through the crowd to show off while others cooed and reached out to pet her. This time, she wasn't the only one—the other humans got the same treatment throughout the club. Some were perched in their client's laps or sitting with them in the steaming lounge pools to be further doted on. A few lizards fed Aster little treats that turned out to be a popular type of human candy, which she feigned gratefulness for, trying to turn off the part of her brain that was still weirded out (and a little mortified).

"*So cute,*" one lizard grunted, touching her cheek with a scaly knuckle.

"Th-thank you!" Aster answered awkwardly.

Eventually, the lizards began to lead their respective humans to the cages, and Aster ended up next to Joely—who gave her an open-mouth smile and waved with both hands. Aster waved back.

The rest of the night went pretty much how she expected, with the drinks-poured-over-the-cages routine. When Aster was led to a private booth and tipped at fifteen percent, she managed a little happy dance that would be blackmail material if anyone recorded it. *Fuck, hopefully no one is filming any of this,* she thought as she was once again slurped to oblivion by her client's long tongue.

When the group was back outside, Joely found her first. Her green bangs, saturated with saliva, were plastered to her forehead.

"Hey! You came back!"

"Hey! Yeah, I did."

"They had *good* candy tonight," she said dreamily. "Are you coming with us to Zion this time?"

A few others joined them.

"Ah, shit yeah, Zion," one added.

"Hey, Juniper," Joely responded to the person wearing a fuzzy orange leotard and white combat boots. "You look cute in that."

Belatedly, Aster realized that Patrek was standing beside her and nodded in greeting.

"So, you coming?" he asked.

"Sure," Aster said. "Why not?"

Joely and a few others cheered out loud at her response. Aster had to laugh at their enthusiasm for a near-stranger joining them.

The group boarded a train together, and during the ride, most of them took the same orange pills from last time. Aside from Aster, Patrek was the only one who declined—Aster got the sense that he preferred to stay alert.

"What are those, anyway?" Aster asked as Joely put away the pill pack.

"Pure joy," she said. As the train passed through a dim tunnel, Aster could see that her pupils—and the pupils of everyone else who took the pills—were glowing blue.

"Joely, how many did you take?" Patrek asked.

"Who knows!" she said, throwing out her arms and leaving them there.

"Be careful on the dance floor, okay?"

In reply, Joely dropped her arms and hugged him. "Yes, Father."

As they reached their stop, Juniper, who had been mostly quiet, stepped up beside Aster. "Just so you know, don't tell anyone in there that you're a pet. Lots of people don't, uh, react that well."

"A . . . pet?"

"Well yeah," they answered, brows furrowed. "What else would you call it?"

Departing the train, the group only had to walk across the street to enter Zion. Near the door, Aster's feed pinged with an available map, which confused her until she realized it was the layout of the club. She waved it off, wondering why a club would even need a map—which was answered moments later when they stepped inside.

Aster froze in place. "Holy fucking stars."

The room itself might have been the largest one she had ever seen, and "the dance floor" was at least five different sections across multiple levels. The massive crowd was visible in flashes, as sets of lights strobed with the beat. On the full back wall of the club was an enormous projection of Freyja, the orangey brown gas giant that Ascension orbited, and all around the room, colorful holograms shifted and pulsed with the music. It was enough sensory overload that, for several minutes, Aster forgot how to do anything other than stare.

Most of the group eagerly rushed off to join the throng, while Aster and Patrek stood back to observe the spectacle from afar.

"I'm going this way, if you want to join me," Patrick said, gesturing to a plush lounge area that looked far more like Aster's scene.

When they were seated on a fancy sofa moments later, servers offered them drinks from trays. Patrek took one in a tall glass with pink liquid, giving off yellow smoke. An interface bubble next to an identical drink informed Aster that it was called a Flaming Yawn and that she had a coupon for a free drink on her first visit.

Taking one and thanking the server, she took a sip and found it to be citrus-like with fizz and a spicy finish.

"Whoa," she said.

Patrek smiled. "Yeah, they have a kick."

She nodded, taking another sip. "So, how do those lizards have so much money, anyway?"

Patrek swallowed another sip of his drink. "Most of them are very wealthy, yeah. Some are even celebrities in their culture. It's a big status thing that they can afford us, and that we're willing to go along with it . . . Ascension is pretty much the only place they're getting away with a club like that."

"Are you from here?"

He shook his head. "I finished my master's degree at a university on the planet Alviss and decided to be adventurous. I ended up here, and I'm getting a good savings going, so I'm staying a while. You?"

"I was on Victory Station before for a few years, but I . . . needed a change of scenery. My partner and I just relocated here."

"Partner, huh?" he asked, noticeably buzzed now. "Do they know about . . . ?"

"Oh yeah, she knows."

"You could invite her out here."

"Oh no, she has an early morning. She's a doctor."

"Wow," he said, blowing out yellow smoke from his last sip. "That's *groovy*."

Thinking about Cori lying in bed alone evoked an odd emotion. Suddenly, Aster didn't really want to be sitting on this sofa in this noisy club full of pretentious, intoxicated people when she could be resting beside her.

"Are you good if I head out?" she asked, just to be polite, setting her drink aside.

Patrek nodded, unbothered. "Yeah, I think I'm gonna go next door for a massage." He gestured behind him—just beyond the lounge, there was a large archway exit. "The whole block is connected."

"Good call," she said. "Have a nice night."

"You, too."

Back on the train, Aster was glad to be leaving Zion. She

might have enjoyed a place like that when she was younger—*maybe*—but now it was just exhausting. Plus, even though she had Cori's blessing to go out and party, she couldn't shake a weird, guilty feeling about staying out so late.

✳ ✳ ✳

Back at the condo, Aster attempted to shower and dry off as quickly as possible, then climbed into bed next to Cori in the dark bedroom.

"Hi," Cori said softly, pulling her into her arms. "Did you have a good night?"

"Yeah." Aster curled into her. "We went to Zion. Glad to be back."

They kissed once and then Cori was still again. It took longer for Aster to fall asleep, but after she did, it felt like only moments had passed when Cori's alarm woke them up. Aster got up with her to fix breakfast. As she was preparing some toast, Cori's arms found their way around her waist from behind.

"Thank you," she said.

"Of course." Aster swiveled around to kiss her.

"You must be tired."

Aster shrugged. "I wanted to see you. I missed you last night."

They kissed again.

"How was the club?"

"Oh, it was unreal... Just, the most ridiculous club I've ever seen. I don't even know how to explain it."

Cori laughed. "Sounds memorable, at least!"

"I guess that's true. I won't be out that long all the time, though."

"But you said you had fun, right?"

"Yeah... I mean, it was an experience. Not really my scene, though."

"Well, I'm glad you had an adventure. Maybe you'll find more things here you *do* like."

"Maybe," Aster allowed.

After they ate, Cori was off to work, and Aster fell promptly back into bed, sleeping well past midday.

When she woke up again, she stood up and stretched, reflecting on how nice it was to not be in pain after a work night. Next, she submitted her payment, watching as the module blinked and recalculated her remaining debt.

She had been so afraid to leave Victory that it was surreal to think that she'd lucked out so quickly here and found a new, safer way to make money. But she knew better than to get comfortable—the lizard club was a good option for now, but that type of establishment might not be destined to last.

Passing by their unused treatment room on her way to the kitchen, Aster felt a silly tug of nostalgia for the way Cori used to tend to her. It was how they met, after all. Anytime Aster had returned with even the slightest injury, Cori had been there to soothe her, keeping her calm and comfortable while she assessed the damage. Maybe Cori missed the emotional aspects of that care, in some way, as well. Even if she'd never admit it.

That gave Aster an idea.

✯ ✯ ✯

Aster had dinner ready by the time Cori got back from work. While they ate, she told her about Zion, as best as she could describe it.

"So it sounds like you *did* enjoy it," Cori said.

Aster shrugged. "It was worth seeing once."

Afterward, when they had cleared the table, Cori pressed a kiss to Aster's neck and ran her thumb across her skin there.

"Are you sore at all? From the collar?"

Completely by accident, she had given Aster a perfect segue into her next request.

"No, not my neck. But my back and shoulders are actually a little tight. I thought maybe a massage—"

"Oh, yes, of course!" Cori said, with palpable delight. "Come lie down."

Moments later, Aster was lying face down on the treatment bed, Cori's hands gliding across her skin, rubbing and pressing—making good use of a nice lotion Aster picked up at the market earlier.

"You *do* have lots of tension," Cori said. "I'm sorry we've never done this before."

Aster was already so blissed out, melting into the bed at Cori's touch, that it took her a moment to process the words.

"If I'd known you were so good at it . . ." she mumbled.

Cori squeezed her shoulder. "I'm glad you think so."

Her strong hands were gentle but firm, finding each knot and easing out the tightness in a deeply pleasant way, traveling first across Aster's back and then up to her neck and down each arm. By the time Cori paused to clean her hands, Aster couldn't quite remember her own name.

Cori returned shortly. Aster felt her let down her hair, raking through it with her fingers and moving to lightly massage Aster's scalp with small circular motions. It felt so ridiculously nice that Aster nearly laughed, suppressing it at the last second so that Cori wouldn't think anything tickled.

"Your hair is so gorgeous," Cori remarked.

"It matches my mom's," Aster said, rolling over to look at her. "Thank you. That was honestly amazing. Have you been trained in that?"

"Actually, yes, briefly," Cori said, sitting on the bed beside her. "I took a massage therapy course in college . . . Which makes me regret that it never dawned on me to offer you this. It's just been a long time since I've done it."

"My mom—not the same one, one of my other moms—did massages for years," Aster said, fondly recalling how the scent of the oil always lingered on her clothes. "I'd offer to return the favor, but I doubt that I can manage anything that good."

"Oh, that's okay," Cori said, shaking her head. "My body isn't very receptive to the technique, anyway... But I *do* like it when you run your fingers over my back."

Aster smiled and sat up to pull Cori into a kiss, which swiftly gave way to a tight embrace. Aster didn't miss a beat, running her fingers over Cori's back as they held each other. Cori hummed in appreciation—and maybe a little amusement.

"I love you," Aster said.

"I love you, too," Cori said softly.

14

Remember Earth

Thirteen years ago — Earth

Corinth-N was running toward an immobile squadmate when she saw the chopper crash on the shoreline. It was impossible to know if it was a genuine accident or part of the current training exercise, but that was probably the point. Her body responded to the spike in her heart rate by shifting into combat mode, and her chest and limbs pulsed with a sharp surge of raw energy.

At seventeen, her enhancements had been completed two years prior, but she wasn't quite used to that feeling yet, like there was fire in her veins that might consume her if she didn't complete her current task. The heavy boots of her combat armor were turning rubble into dust with each impact—drowned out by the voices of the rest of her team over the comms.

"Shit," was one of the only words she could make out, followed by, "Vehicle down!" and "They're not responding!"

"I'm not far from the shore," she said within her helmet. "But Beirut-H is down."

"Go on," came the reply from Beirut-H. "My armor just locked up and won't reboot—got comms back, at least. Piece of junk."

"Affirmative, Corinth-N, go check the crash for survivors. We'll cover you."

She started toward the wreckage, smoldering bright orange and releasing a plume of smoke into the gray sky, and was able to cover ground twice as fast as usual thanks to being in combat mode. She was getting close when suddenly there was annoying static interference in her visual feed.

"Is anyone else seeing—"

She came to an abrupt halt, falling forward with a hard impact and realizing a moment later that she could no longer move.

"Shit!" she called into her comm. "I'm locked up!"

She tried to tell her suit to reboot, but her visuals were still jumbled. There was brief chaos on the link and then it blinked out, leaving her in complete silence.

"Hello?" she called. "HELLO?"

The next thing she heard was a piercing wail, so high and shrill it felt like her ears would bleed. All she could do was scream.

After what felt like mere minutes, Corinth-N woke

up in an empty room. Her armor was gone, replaced by a chair—to which her arms, ankles, and waist were shackled. At once, she attempted to stand, using an amount of force that should have broken the bonds easily, only to find that they automatically recalibrated and became both thicker and tighter, effectively restraining her in the seat.

This was not Earth tech. She had never seen this before. That could mean only one thing: She had been captured by Mars. At once, she could feel her body on the cusp of slipping into combat mode, which would not help her here. Closing her eyes, she took a few deep breaths to steady her heart.

The door of the small room opened, and a man appeared there on the threshold, coming inside. Corinth-N looked away from him, training her eyes on the floor. She would give him nothing. She would die first.

"Hello there," he said, in an accent she'd never heard. "I'm Lieutenant Roscoe Estrada. You're Corinth, right? Corinth-N?"

She continued staring at the floor. Roscoe crouched before her, right in her line of sight. Corinth-N had never seen a Martian in person before. He had hair on his head and on his face. Strange.

"Listen, you are not a prisoner here. This was a rescue mission. We're trying to get as many of you out as we can before we initiate the next phase. We're taking you to a planet called Idun, where you'll be welcomed as a refugee."

He was attempting to make her disoriented with lies, she knew. Nothing he said made any sense. There was no such thing as a planet called Idun.

"Why would you want to rescue us?" she asked. "What's the next phase?"

"My government is going to eliminate the planet. Not everyone agrees on that choice, but they think it's the only way to end this war. We know it wasn't your fault, though. We know you were forced to fight. The way they treated you was wrong. All of us agree on that."

"You're going to *destroy* Earth?" she asked, feeling a pit in her stomach.

"Yes," he said. "That's why we want to extract as many of you as we can beforehand."

Corinth-N didn't know what to say. This didn't feel like an interrogation. If he didn't want *information* from her, what did he want? If they were really blowing up the planet, that meant Earth had already lost. Why would they bother capturing anyone at all ... unless he was telling the truth about it being a *rescue*?

"I know you're confused," Roscoe went on. "There is a lot they never told you about us, about the reasons the war began. When you get to Idun, you'll be able to go to school and the library, and learn more about our shared history, if you want to."

"Library?" Corinth-N said, curiosity getting the better of her. "Like ... with books?"

"Yes, that's right! Books on any topic you can think of. You could spend hours there and barely make a dent...Now, that's interesting. No one else has ever asked me that."

"Paper books, too? Do they have those?"

"Oh, paper books? You know, I'm not sure. They might have a few in the special collections. But I'll tell you what, if you want to see paper books, you can visit the Museum of Human History. They have some artifacts there that are over two thousand years old."

"What's a *museum*?"

"It's a special building devoted to preserving important things so that people can see them in real life and learn about them ... Here, let me show you some pictures."

Roscoe took out his tablet and tapped it a few times. Corinth-N felt like she was doing something incorrect by talking to him so much, but none of this was anything like her training. And if he *was* trying to trick her, maybe the best strategy would be to let him think it was working.

"Look here," he said, turning the screen toward her. "That's the front of the museum. Really nice architecture. Now, inside—"

He started to swipe the picture, but Corinth-N had only just begun to understand it.

"Wait," she said. "Go back."

He swiped back to show the front of the building again—it wasn't shaped like any building she'd ever seen.

The setting around it was so bright and green. Like an old picture from before the Earth died.

"This planet has *trees*?" she asked, studying the tall plants on either side of the building.

"Yes," Roscoe said with a smile. "Very good eye! There are lots of trees on Idun, and so many other kinds of plants, too. I think you'll really like it there."

All at once, Corinth-N felt like a switch had flipped in her mind. She didn't care if it was a trick. She *wanted* this to be true. She wanted to be going to that place with a library and paper books and real trees. She wanted to believe him.

"How many planets are there?" she asked. "With people living on them?"

"Well, there are twelve in the major worlds. And altogether, there are twenty-seven now."

A strange sound emerged from her mouth, like a cry-laugh. She didn't know what to think anymore. Her whole life, she had been told that it was just Earth and Mars, and that they had to fight to save Earth, or they would never have a green planet again.

"It's going to be okay," Roscoe said, touching her shoulder. "I promise. You're free now. You don't have to fight anymore."

"Do you have any more pictures I can see? Of the planet?"

"I sure do," he said. "I'm going to remove those arm

restraints now, so that you can hold this, but if you try to attack me, we'll have to sedate you. Do you understand?"

Corinth-N nodded, tears falling. "I don't want to hurt you," she said, surprised by how much she meant it. "I don't want to hurt you."

"Good," he said. "That's something we have in common."

✳ ✳ ✳

Present

After a month in her new clinic, Cori was enjoying the variety of patients on Ascension. Here, people often arrived wearing party clothes with various substances still in their systems, injured during what was supposed to be a night of fun. Some patients would maintain a positive attitude through their appointment, joking about what went wrong, while others were just annoyed at having their vacation interrupted.

Regardless of their disposition when they arrived, though, Cori was happy to find that most of them were in high spirits by the time their treatment was complete—but maybe it was no wonder, when the station itself had such a joyful vibe.

Most of the time, anyway.

Passing down a hallway with large windows that overlooked the courtyard, Cori found a cluster of other medical staff watching something below. She stepped over to join the mass and was surprised to see some sort of protest demonstration—a small crowd of people holding signs and chanting. Realization dawned when she noticed that several of the signs showed images of Earth. The crowd's current chant was *We won't forget*. It was the anniversary of the planet's destruction, of course. Somehow, the date always snuck up on her.

"Do they really think that's going to accomplish anything?" someone wondered out loud.

"They're right," another responded. "We can't just forget what Mars did."

A few people moved on, apparently perturbed by one opinion or the other. Cori stayed looking at the crowd for a moment longer and then continued on her way, promptly engaged by a nurse with questions.

She had nearly forgotten the demonstration altogether—until that evening at dinner.

"So, apparently, I need new clothes," Aster reported as they ate, "if you'd like to spend your day off shopping with me?"

"Absolutely!" Cori responded, happy at the thought of exploring more of the station together.

"Did you ... see that Remember Earth group protesting today?" Aster asked, oddly cautious.

"I did, from above."

"I was wondering what you think of it."

Cori shook her head. "Think of what?"

"Their position. That the Martian government shouldn't be allowed to represent humanity."

"Oh," Cori said, sipping her wine and taking a moment to think. "You may already know this, but the people who rescued me *were* Martian. So, I think the protesters mean well, and I can understand their point of view, but I also don't think Earth gave Mars any other options. They repeatedly refused to surrender, and Mars had the bigger guns. The end became inevitable. The 'leaders' we had weren't interested in peace, only in winning—so I can't say an alternate outcome would have been any better."

Aster nodded as she took another bite.

"What do *you* think?" Cori asked after a moment.

"I'm never really sure what to think, to be honest. It all feels so far removed from my life and weirdly personal at the same time . . . I do think it's important to keep the memory alive. Like you said before. So that we don't forget our past."

"Although, sometimes I do wonder if we've truly learned anything," Cori said. "Sometimes it seems unlikely that our species will ever evolve beyond its inclination toward violence. But I know that sounds cynical."

"No, I understand. I mean, I *think* I do. Not that I could ever really understand what it was like."

Cori met her gaze. "I'm glad you don't. I wouldn't wish it on anyone."

Aster looked thoughtful and ate quietly for a moment before a smile spread over her face.

"What is it?"

"Oh, nothing. I was just thinking, you'd probably like Centauride. Where I grew up."

Cori smiled back. "I'd *love* to see it someday."

"I'd love to take you there," Aster agreed. "Someday."

✹ ✹ ✹

The following day, they fell upon a fraction of the hundreds of clothing stores the station had to offer. While Aster didn't seem to be having much fun trying on a kaleidoscope of colorful outfits, Cori found that *watching* her was thoroughly enjoyable.

When Aster stepped out in a gold wig, a glowing strapless top that hugged her torso, and glittery black shorts, looking deeply skeptical, Cori applauded in encouragement. "You look fantastic!"

"Are you *sure*?" she asked, turning around in front of the mirror nook. "Hmm ... I guess it's not bad."

"Is it comfortable enough to wear out afterward, too?"

Aster shrugged. "I don't think I'll be going out much."

"You might change your mind."

"I doubt it. But it's fine for whatever, I guess."

After she was back in her own clothes, Aster gathered Cori into her arms, adding, "I don't need anyone but you."

Cori had more to say, but for now, she smiled and pulled Aster into a kiss.

After Aster had acquired several new outfits, they stopped at a "cafe" for lunch, which looked more like a palace built for ancient royalty, with marble-esque floors, gold columns, and the faint melody of instrumental music.

At one point, a group of people with balloon hats came noisily in and took a table on the balcony above them, toasting drinks and cheering. Cori smiled to see their happy gathering, but Aster rolled her eyes.

"It's kind of nice, isn't it?" Cori asked. "To be in a place with so much joy."

"I guess." Aster shrugged. "It's just a *loud* type of joy."

Cori laughed. "True. Hey, is this a bad time for a serious question?"

"Shoot."

"Do you think it's possible that you've been on your own so long that the idea of new friendships feels . . . dangerous to you?"

Aster gave her a look. "Holy stars, Cori, are you a *psychiatrist*, too?"

"No, I've just been to therapy."

"Oh." Aster looked down and sighed. "I don't know. Maybe. At that dance club, I just . . . I felt out of place, and then I missed you."

Cori took her hand. "You can always come back if you're not enjoying it. But I don't want you to think you're doing anything *wrong* by going out and having fun. Maybe these people aren't the *right* people, but it's impossible to know without giving them a chance, right? Just a thought."

Aster still looked somber. "I *was* alone for a long time."

"I know."

"The last person... The last person I was close to was my ex, and I wouldn't call that much of a friendship. He didn't stay around long after I started working off the debt."

"Oh," Cori said, heart sinking. "Back when you told me what you were afraid might happen between us, I didn't even realize—"

"No!" Aster said, interrupting. "That wasn't what happened with him. At all. He wasn't *worried* about me. He was... disgusted. And jealous."

Cori had rarely hated a stranger so quickly. "How cruel of him."

"That's a good word for what he was. I'm... Ugh, I'm sorry. I don't mean to be talking about this so much. Is this weird?"

"Of course not. You can tell me anything." Cori pulled her into a partial embrace and kissed her cheek. "I'm not saying that you should go out and do anything you don't *want* to do, okay? But I hope you'll keep an open mind. To new adventures and new people."

"You're right. As usual."

Cori barked a laugh. "Let's not get carried away."

As they finished their sandwiches, Aster seemed lost in

thought. Cori said nothing more on the topic, giving her time to reflect.

> * * *

Aster never expected to understand what Joely meant when she said she was "jealous" of her first time, but after just a couple weeks, the absurdity had faded into monotony. Still, compared to her old gig, that was a welcome change. Unlike her clients on Victory, none of the Umblyrhyn ever handled her too roughly or gave her any reasons to feel unsafe.

One night, as she approached the club, she realized something was different: Instead of lining up, the other people were standing around and talking—and two lizards were cleaning something off the side of the club, illuminating the wall with a lamp and applying a white foam.

"What's going on?" Aster asked, finding Patrek in the group.

"They're just getting rid of some graffiti tags before they open. Apparently someone went around throwing programmed paint darts at a few places around here."

Aster glanced back at the club and did a double take when she caught sight of the piece of graffiti currently lit by the lamp: Three blue rectangles.

"That symbol," she said, "I've seen it before, on Victory Station."

Patrek nodded without needing to ask what she meant. "Want to go for a walk?"

"Sure," Aster said, intrigued.

They started down the block together, passing a couple other clubs before Patrek spoke. "There's an extremist group called Humanity First. Heard of them?"

Aster shook her head.

"They're pretty fringe, and for good reason. They see other species as inherently inferior, so any place that has humans and aliens mingling is something they see as a *threat* to our kind."

Aster scoffed. "How does that make any sense? When they've all been around *longer* than us?"

"It doesn't. It makes no sense. Their position is that humans are superior, but everything they do demonstrates the opposite. There's zero logic to it."

"How do you know so much about them?" she asked.

"Seven years ago," Patrek started, avoiding eye contact, "they recruited my sister. She's fine now—better than fine; she's back on our home planet teaching music. But when she got involved with them, it was like...she became someone else. The things she said, the way she was so angry all the time. If they could get to someone like her...they must be very persuasive."

"I'm glad she's doing better," Aster said.

"Me, too."

They had reached the end of the block and turned around, heading back to the lizard club.

"I didn't know if I'd see any evidence of them on this station, but honestly, I'm not surprised," Patrek went on. "Where did you see the symbol on Victory? If you don't mind saying."

"I ran into a group of them—they had matching tattoos. It was right before Human New Year, actually, so they were probably passing through."

Patrek hummed at that. "Did they give you any trouble?"

"Well...yes. It was late and I was walking home alone, and they accused me of being an escort."

Patrek stopped and looked at her with wide eyes.

"It went about how you'd expect."

"Fuck," he muttered, shaking his head. "Hey, I'm glad you're okay, too."

"Thanks. Me, too."

They reached the club shortly, which was now open for business as usual—the clients were making their selections of human pets for the night.

"You still down?" Patrek asked.

"Oh, heck yeah. Let's piss off some cultists."

He laughed at that, clapped his hands, and they took their places in line.

Aster was getting better at recognizing the regulars, though she didn't know their names or genders—very few of them had public profiles—and the only consistent difference in treatment when she was chosen by a new visitor was that they were typically more generous with tipping.

Each client was a little different. Some really got into the part where they walked her around for their peers to see, while others preferred to dote on her by themselves. Some clearly enjoyed the cage/drink thing, while others seemed to just be going along with tradition. Some were methodical when it came to the licking, as though they were genuinely trying to "clean" her, while others were much more chaotic and hastier.

At the end of the night, when Joely was handing out pills as usual, Aster decided to be adventurous.

"Why not?" she said, taking one.

Joely's eyes lit up and she stepped closer. "Welcome. To *heaven*."

It took a while to kick in, but by the time Aster stepped off the train at Zion, the whole world had gone soft and glowy around her. Everything looked warm, welcoming, *beautiful*. Walking (floating?) into the club was like entering a higher realm of happy souls, all connected by music and emotion and thriving on the very pulse of the universe. At once, Aster was *exploding* with the energy of being alive. She *needed* to join in this important celebration with everyone who was lucky enough to *exist*. This had been the *point* of everything all along; she just couldn't see until now. She looked up at one point and cried actual tears at the sight of a blooming flower hologram, thinking it was the most perfect thing she had ever witnessed and clearly held the *meaning* of life within its unfurling petals, until Patrek grabbed her arm to snap her out of it.

"Hey," she said, still weeping. "You have nice eyelashes."

"Okay, let's take a break," he said, pulling her toward the lounge.

When she woke up the next day with a fuzzy headache and heavy limbs, she decided that the drug would not be something she made a habit of.

15
The Beach

Just over two months into life on Ascension, another night began normally enough. Aster was chosen by a client she'd had once before, a slightly shy lizard who liked to feed her chocolate crackers from a package, which were honestly really tasty. The client smiled and petted her hair—dyed purple for the night—after she munched each one.

As she was being led to a cage, there was a scream somewhere behind them. Aster turned to see that, across the room, Joely had a bloody gash across her face. Before Aster could fully process what was going on, her client dropped her leash and rushed over, joined by several others who ganged up on a specific lizard and forced them from the building, angrily growling all the while. The sounds made Aster's blood go cold. She had never heard any of the Umblyrhyn sound so *ferocious*.

After the offending lizard had been booted, Aster's client

rushed back through the crowd, shoving their way over to Joely. Aster couldn't see what happened next, since Joely was obscured by a swarm of concerned lizards, now sadly cooing, all anger evaporated.

Eventually, the swarm eased up, and a few lizards walked Joely over to the door. Aster's client came back, then, and spoke to her—she could hear others doing the same.

Violence is forbidden, came the auto-translation in her feed as they grunted. *You are safe here. Please do not be afraid. We conclude the night early, so you may aid the injured friend.*

Just like that, they removed Aster's collar.

"Thank you," she said, because she couldn't think of anything else. Her client nodded.

Outside, the group found Joely sitting on a bench and sucking a gas dart, blood smeared all over her face from the licking. The gash, starting at her brow and ending by her nostril, was still actively leaking blood down her chin and onto her shirt.

"Oh shit, Joely," Patrek said, wincing.

"We should get you to a clinic," Aster said.

That got her a cold glare. "And tell them *what* when they ask how I got this?"

"Let's at least go to a pharmacy and get some bandages," Patrek offered.

Aster had another idea. She stepped to the side and called Cori via the interface to check in first—she was shocked that

Aster thought she needed to ask. "Bring her here immediately!" she half shouted.

Aster smiled and disconnected. "I think I can help," she told the group. "My partner is a doctor, and we have a private treatment suite in our apartment. We can go there now."

Patrek met her gaze and smiled.

"Why not *lead* with that?" Joely asked, hopping up.

They boarded a train together, taking turns supporting Joely as they walked. When they were seated, Aster ended up across from her. Joely was impressively serene for someone who had been clawed in the face.

"You had Nylina tonight," Joely said, smiling dreamily. "I love her . . . She always has treats."

"How do you know her name?" Aster asked.

"I asked her," she said softly. "I told her mine, too. She's . . . she's my favorite."

When they arrived at the condo, Cori greeted them at the door. The whole group poured into the treatment room, where they helped Joely get situated on the bed. Cori was already in doctor mode, speaking to her in a reassuring way and administering pain meds before she scanned her face. The wound was wide enough that she applied temporary adhesive stitches before setting up the healing lamp—which made the ones on Victory look *ancient*. Instead of a simple percentage meter on the top, this one had a screen that adjusted in size and shape with the rest of the device, forming an oval over Joely's face and displaying a detailed render of the wound being repaired in real time.

Seeing Cori with another patient filled Aster with pride. Cori was so compassionate, so naturally suited to her work. By the time she had Joely in a brace to keep her head still beneath the healing lamp, Joely was fully relaxed—maybe even asleep.

Cori turned to face the group. "While we wait, does anyone else need my help?"

Aster hadn't even considered that others in the group might be hurt. But, right away, Juniper stepped forward. "I actually have a rash," they said, somewhat hesitantly. "It's probably no big deal, but . . ."

"Let me take a look," Cori said, motioning them closer and examining their torso where they had raised their top.

From where she was standing, Aster could see that the skin on their abdomen was red and flaking. Their arms and face looked a little rosy, too.

"This looks like an allergic reaction," Cori said. "Could it be from the Umblyrhyn saliva?"

A few people's eyes went wide as saucers, and someone let out a nervous laugh.

"Hey, it's okay, she knows everything!" Aster said, realizing she should have mentioned that before.

Now less hesitant, Juniper started giving more details about how the rash always happened after the lizards licked them, and how it usually itched for a few days and then faded away. Cori listened closely, then gave them an antihistamine stamp for the itching and a cream for the inflammation. For long-term help, she said she'd submit a prescription for an allergy med and advised them to take it before each work night.

After that, several people started talking at once, suddenly eager to get a doctor's advice. Cori addressed them one by one, complimenting their outfits and speaking with them as though they were already her friends, while regularly turning back to Joely to be sure she was doing alright.

Aster caught Cori's eye at one point and smiled in a way that she hoped conveyed how proud she was. She could tell she had succeeded when Cori seemed the tiniest bit flustered for a moment, stumbling over the word "medication."

That's my future wife, Aster thought, grinning. *How the heck did I get so lucky?*

When Joely sat up to face the group, she looked like herself again, minus her typical makeup. The group rejoiced to see her fully healed.

"This calls for a celebration," someone said, prompting a few laughs.

With all patients treated, Aster could finally move over to Cori and slip her arm around her waist, both facing the group.

"What do you think, Joely?" Patrek asked. "You want to go out or go home?"

Joely sat up a bit straighter and narrowed her eyes as

she thought, humming and clearly relishing the suspense. "I want to go ... to the *beach*."

After a beat, the group agreed with enthusiasm, possibly lacking the courage to argue.

"You guys coming?" Patrek asked.

Before Aster could decline, ready for some time alone with her amazing partner, Cori turned to her and smiled. "The beach sounds fun, right?"

So they went to the beach.

It was a full zone converted to look like a seaside resort, complete with "ocean" waves that lapped at the pale sand and a simulated horizon that followed the cycle lighting. When they arrived, the first whispers of sunrise were starting to color the dark "sky."

Aster had never seen a real horizon *or* a simulated one, so she was mesmerized at first. The longer she stared, though, the less she believed it.

The place wasn't crowded so early in the morning, and the group found some empty volleyball nets next to a bar called Lulu's Luau Hideaway. Aster and Patrek naturally drifted over to the porch to observe, taking advantage of the breakfast buffet to enjoy some fruit smoothies and muffins. Patrek's hair was dyed fuchsia for the evening, which looked almost neon in the golden glow of the simulated sunrise.

They watched as the group began their first game, and Cori hit the ball over the net and celebrated by throwing her hands up.

"She seems great," Patrek observed.

Aster nodded. "She's the best."

"That was very generous, what she did for everyone."

"She would disagree."

Patrek discarded a melon wedge from the top of his drink and took a long sip. "How did you two meet?"

"She was a doctor on Victory, and I was a frequent patient... Very frequent, since I *was* actually escorting there for a while."

His smile dropped. "Oh, shit. Bet you were glad to get out of there. Then again, I guess *most* people are pretty glad to not be on Victory, huh?"

"I take it you've been."

"Oh, no, I've just heard... uh, heard things about it."

The other side scored in the volleyball game. While they celebrated, Cori clapped for them, too.

"Well, I'm sure what you've heard is true. And yes, I'm very glad we relocated."

"So... first that, now this. Can I ask why?"

"I'm in debt," Aster said with a shrug.

His eyebrows shot up. "That must be one fucking motherload of debt."

"Don't ever take a smuggling job."

"Good advice. Thanks."

The pity in his eyes made her itchy. Thankfully, a distraction came.

"Aster!" Cori called out, facing the bar. "Come play one with us?"

Aster smiled, finished her drink, and stood. She shot Patrek one last look and found the same subtle sympathy on his face, which made her glad to be walking away from wherever that conversation was headed.

She slipped off her shoes and stepped into the soft sand, taking her place on Cori's side of the net. The game that followed was pure chaos. It didn't seem like anyone knew the rules, but it *was* fun—especially since Cori looked so happy. After a while, Patrek joined them, too, and the rest of the "match" was a flurry of sand and wild laughter.

Aster and Cori were first to leave; it was getting close to the time when Cori needed to get ready for her shift. They waved to the whole group before departing.

As they headed back toward the train station, Aster turned to take one last look at the simulated sky, now painted with the bright colors of a sunrise.

"Is it *really* like that?" she asked.

"Sometimes," Cori said, and they joined hands as they continued on. "I'd love to show you the real thing, someday. If you like."

Aster paused before she responded. A long time ago, she had promised one of her mothers that no matter where her travels took her, she would never set foot on a planet. Too many things could go wrong, her mother had warned—atmospheres were unpredictable, and the native flora and fauna could be dangerous to humans. Best to stay on stations, in the homes humans created for themselves.

It was a promise Aster had managed to keep so far. But she decided she didn't really want to talk about all that right now. "I'd go anywhere with you," she said, giving Cori's hand a squeeze.

Seated on the train moments later, Cori admired the lei she was still wearing. "That was fun."

"Yeah, it was," Aster agreed.

"Your friend Patrek seems nice."

"Yeah, he is. He's fun to talk to. And he looks out for the others. I think he feels protective of them."

"He's a Believer."

"Oh, I don't know if—"

Cori nodded. "I saw him circle his heart when you all arrived at the condo earlier."

"Huh. He's never mentioned it." Aster yawned, ready to sleep for a long time. She was a little sad Cori couldn't come to bed with her when they got home.

"I'm really glad to have met them," Cori added.

"Me, too."

16

Safety

Sitting bored in her cage at the lizard club, Aster's thoughts drifted to that beach trip the week before. Cori was still talking about how much fun she had with the group, and Aster was glad that living on this station had turned out to be so much better than she expected.

She was shaken out of her daydream by a faint rumble and the sound of shouting. Looking around, she couldn't see anything out of the ordinary in the club, but she could tell the people on either side of her heard it, too.

Only a few moments later, there was a second rumble, and then a third, close enough to shake the walls. Someone screamed. Aster could smell smoke. Snapping into action, she unclasped her leash and exited her cage, helping a few other people do the same. The club lights came on and the music stopped. Everyone was quickly pouring toward a back exit Aster hadn't seen before.

The next rumble came as a boom that threw her off balance and knocked pieces of the ceiling loose. Chaos followed—some of the lizards were trying to help the humans leave in an orderly fashion, while the others were more preoccupied with getting the fuck out of there.

But what was even going on?

The back exit led them to a tunnel passage, which then spit them into a secluded area a couple blocks away from the club. Apparently the lizards knew it well; it made sense that they might want to be discreet as they came and went.

Somewhere in the panicked crowds, Aster could hear some kind of siren—and more screaming. A haze of smoke hung in the air, and people were running down the pathways in every direction.

"Oh, shit," Patrek said, the color draining from his face. "The *network* is down."

Belatedly, Aster realized he was right: her interface access had already blinked out, the contacts rendered useless. It was also getting brighter—the station lighting was shifting to emergency daylight.

"What the fuck is happening?" someone else wondered out loud.

Joely was curled up in the lap of a lizard who was petting her hair. Someone else was physically ill nearby. Everyone was nervous and confused. Several of the lizards left in haste, but a few stayed behind, apparently indecisive.

Aster was anxious. She wanted to get in touch with Cori,

to let her know she was alright, but there was no telling how long the network would be down. The fact that it hadn't been restored yet suggested that this wasn't just a random glitch, which was an unsettling thought.

"Hey," Patrek said, suddenly beside her. "You alright?"

"Yeah, I'm good. I just . . . I wish I could message Cori. She'll be so worried."

"Go on home. Just be careful out there."

Aster looked over at the others. A few were so young. They might need help.

"I'll stay with them," Patrek added. "You go on."

"As soon as comms are back—"

"I'll message you."

"Thank you," she said.

The train platform was a jam-packed nightmare, and Aster really didn't want to go so far on foot, so she considered the painful purchase of a hovercab ticket . . . only to realize that air travel had been stalled.

Accepting her fate and settling for a long walk, Aster was able to move with the crowds most of the time, sometimes darting onto less busy avenues when she could. The people around her were loud, and her body was tense with the knowledge that more danger might arise at any moment.

When she reached a human-dominant zone, she managed to find a platform that wasn't quite as bad, so she boarded a train for the rest of the trip, repeatedly trying her useless feed. All the screens in the train had been switched to an emergency message instructing passengers to return to their residences immediately. In the back of her mind, she wondered if *anything* on this scale had ever happened here before.

By the time she made it to the apartment, nearly two hours had passed since the first rumble. She had to scan her wrist chip at a security checkpoint to enter, and then she was *finally* on the elevator.

Cori's arms were around her as soon as she put one foot through the door. "Aster!" Cori cried, pulling her close.

In the quiet safety of their condo, Aster realized how much her own heart was pounding. "I'm here. I'm alright."

"They have the building under lockdown, so I couldn't come find you."

"I got here as fast as I could."

In reply, Cori hugged her tighter—a little *too* tightly, which made Aster squeak without meaning to.

"Sorry," Cori said, easing off. "Did that hurt? I'm sorry."

"No, I'm fine," Aster said. Then she realized she could hear something strange, like a faint whirring sound...coming from Cori's chest.

"What is that? Are *you* okay?"

Cori nodded. "I shifted into combat mode—it's a bit like an adrenaline spike—but I'm coming down. That hasn't happened in a long time. I wasn't sure it was still possible."

Aster reached out and rubbed her shoulder. "I'm *so* sorry."

Cori sighed and moved to kiss her, gently. "Not your fault. I'm so glad you're back. Unfortunately, I do need to go downstairs. I'm sure they could use help."

"Of course."

"Will you stay in for now? I mean, even if they lift the warnings. Just ... please don't go back out there."

"I won't. I promise. I'll be right here. You don't have to worry anymore."

"Thank you," Cori said.

After she donned her uniform and pulled Aster into one more long embrace, Cori disappeared down to the clinic.

With her nerves too fried to sleep and the network still down, Aster decided to clean the condo as a distraction. It was impossible to do that without thinking of her birth mother, who would reliably start tidying anytime she was stressed.

Sometime later, the network was partially restored, enough to allow an emergency news stream. Aster was quickly glued to the live feed via the massive wall screen. They were reporting that dozens of alien-run attractions had been attacked by some faction of human terrorists. The culprits were still unknown, according to the anchor, but Aster had a pit in her stomach. As they awaited more information, they cycled through images of the damage throughout the station, calling it the worst attack in Ascension's history.

Some time later, news broke that a Remember Earth representative had publicly denounced the attacks, stating that their group stood in solidarity with the victims and that all violence was incompatible with their position.

After that, communication was restored and the lockdown semi-lifted, though all docking ports were still closed. Aster was glad to hear from Patrek that everyone was fine. She also tapped Cori's feed and sent her a string of hearts, so she could have some comfort in her next free moment.

By late morning, there came the update she'd been expecting: Several members of the extremist organization Humanity First had been apprehended. The news didn't identify them or show their faces, but they did show the rectangle trio symbol, noting that any display of that graphic was prohibited station-wide and that sightings of it should be reported immediately.

***

Sometime later, Aster woke up to find Cori smiling at her.

"Hi!" Aster said, getting up and hugging her. "What time is it? Are you back?"

"Just for a few minutes, unfortunately. I wanted to come see how you were doing."

"I'm alright," Aster said. "At least they found the people who did it."

Cori nodded. "Listen, it sounds like everything has settled down out there, so don't feel like you have to stay cooped up all day, alright?"

"Are you sure?"

"Yeah, I'm sure. Are your friends okay?"

"I heard from Patrek after the comms came back—they're good."

"Oh, good. Alright. Well, I better head back."

After saying goodbye for the second time, Aster felt restless—and hungry—so she headed out of the apartment to find some food nearby. Things were mostly back to normal, and she ate on the terrace of a cafe. Afterward, another message from Patrek popped up: he was meeting a few others near the club to see the damage in person. Aster had a fleeting moment of confusion before she realized she wanted to see, too.

When she got there, she did a double take at the little building in shambles, with two walls fully caved in and *CLOSED* holograms activated. Suddenly, it hit her that this incident had serious personal ramifications. She had lost *another* source of revenue and finding a new one on Ascension would now be more difficult.

"Lots of them are in worse shape than this," came Patrek's voice beside her.

He was dressed more casually, and his hair was his natural shade—in the daylight, she could see that it was reddish-brown. She had never really noticed before, but they almost looked like they could be related.

"Has that cult ever done anything else like this?"

"Not on this scale," he said. "Honestly, I'm glad more

people will be aware of them now. I mean, I hate that *this* is what it took."

"We were pretty lucky. Since all we lost was a sweet gig."

"What's next for you?"

"I don't know. I'll have to find new work. Maybe relocate again. You?"

"Back to graduate school."

She gave him a look. "I thought you already finished?"

"Not quite. I'm actually still working on my thesis... in Interspecies Sociology."

He had a twinkle in his eye. Aster connected the dots. "Well done. You must have a wealth of good material now."

"I'm feeling pretty confident. But, uh, the others don't know about that, so."

"Your secret's safe with me."

"Thank you," he said. "I'm glad we met."

"Me, too."

"In fact," he said, suddenly more serious. "I think I was meant to meet you. I've saved up a lot of money working here, and it's way more than I need on Alviss."

Aster was already shaking her head.

"Let me explain. After my sister got mixed up with the wrong people, she vanished. No contact. And then, when she realized she wanted to get out, someone helped her. That's the only reason she made it back home. I'll never meet that person or thank them, but what I *can* do is help you, now that the universe has given me the chance."

"Patrek... I can't take your money."

He gave her a pointed look. "Do you think Cori would let me give it to her?"

Aster looked away for a moment. They both knew the answer.

"I know I probably can't cover everything you owe, but let me help."

Before Aster could answer, someone else was beside them. "You can have mine, too." It was Joely, with rumpled hair and no makeup. She looked oddly happy. "I won't need it where I'm going."

"Where are you going?" Patrek asked.

Joely smiled in a slightly bashful way. "Nylina asked me to come with her to Krystath, her homeworld... and I said yes."

"Joely," Patrek said with alarm, "you *can't* be serious."

"I am, and I don't need your permission," she snapped back. "I like her. It's not like I have anywhere else to go."

"Yes, you do. Come with me to Alviss."

She scoffed.

"I mean it. Lots of great opportunities there. I'll help you decide."

Joely's expression relaxed. "That's sweet, but I'm going to go with her. The humans there... they have *good* lives. They take really good care of them, and they even have these little parties where we all get to see each other and have treats." She grinned like her dreams had come true.

"Are you sure it's what you want?" Patrek asked, more gently now.

Joely nodded, eyes glistening. "I'm so happy she wants *me*."

As if on cue, there was a low grunt nearby, and Aster spotted a lizard waiting at the bottom of the steps.

"Okay, she's here. Give me your code," Joely said, gesturing impatiently.

Aster hesitated.

"Hurry up!"

Aster sent her the code through the feed, and without even a second of hesitation, Joely poked around at the air and transferred a startlingly large sum into Aster's account.

"That's pretty good, considering how much I spent on drugs," she said with a laugh.

"I don't know how to thank you," Aster said. Her voice sounded weird. Like she was under water.

Joely shrugged. "For what? Tell your girlfriend thanks for fixing my face." With a wink and a wave, Joely went bounding down the steps to Nylina, and they joined hands as they walked away together.

"That's good for her, I guess," Aster said to fill the silence.

"How much is left?" Patrek asked.

She gave him a look.

"Aster, please just tell me how much you still owe."

With a heavy sigh, she took out her comm to pull up the account—she didn't want to access it via the interface—and paused a moment before loading Joely's funds into it. It felt absurd to do that so soon, even though she knew she would never see her again.

That brought her debt down so significantly that her eyes went a little blurry and she barked a laugh. She showed the screen to Patrek, who read it and smiled.

"Account number?"

When the next transfer was done, the amount cleared, and that panel vanished from her comm, replaced by an error message stating the account was closed.

"Shit," she said, hands shaking. "This doesn't feel real."

"It's real. You don't have to put yourself through this anymore."

Unable to speak or think, she threw her arms around him, completely unsure if that was weird but not caring. "Thank you."

"You're welcome," he said, hugging her back tightly. "I'm so glad we could help you."

"Cori will be grateful to you, too; she'd want to tell you, she'd want you to know—" Aster rambled and stopped short, tears flowing.

"Give her my best," he said. "And take good care of yourself."

"You, too. You, too."

✳ ✳ ✳

Between patients at the clinic, Cori stepped into her office for a reprieve and found Aster waiting there, leaning against the desk.

"Hi!" Cori said. "Everything alright?"

"Yeah," Aster said, pulling her into a hug. "It is."

Cori eagerly returned the embrace. They didn't let go for a while.

"Actually, everything is . . . better than alright. I had to come tell you something in person."

"Oh?" Cori asked, belatedly realizing that Aster's eyes were red. "What is it?"

Aster shook her head, lip trembling. "It's done. It's over. Joely and Patrek, they—" Her sentence was cut short as her voice wavered. Cori rubbed her back, waiting for her to continue. "They covered the rest of my debt with the money they made at the club," Aster finally explained.

"What?" Cori said, even though she heard her perfectly.

"It's paid off. It's done. I'm free."

"Aster!" she cried, throwing her arms around her again. "Are they here?!"

Aster smiled. "No. They're gone. They both had places to be. Patrek—it was his idea in the first place. I told him you'd be grateful, too."

"Stars above," Cori said, wiping her eyes. "That's wonderful."

"Couldn't have made it this far without you."

They hugged even longer this time.

"I wish I didn't have to go back to work," Cori lamented.

"That's okay. I'm glad I caught you. I'll see you later."

"Yes," Cori said, pulling her into a kiss. "Oh! I guess this means I should . . . give notice? Not to be premature, but I guess we can . . . move on?"

"That sounds good to me."

✳ ✳ ✳

By the time Cori could finally head back to the condo, she was simultaneously exhausted and too giddy to care. When she stepped through the door, Aster swiftly pulled her into her arms and kissed her.

"Hi," Aster said. She looked radiantly happy.

"Hi." Cori kissed her again, lingering.

Aster laughed. "I like where this is going, but how are you not ready to pass out?"

"Hey, I'm way too happy to sleep! Maybe you could . . . help me unwind somehow?"

"Wow," Aster said. "Consider me seduced."

As they made love, Cori relished the feeling of holding Aster so close after such an emotional day. Breathing in the scent of her hair, Cori felt enveloped and let her mind go blank. Nothing existed but the two of them and their bodies and the sounds Aster was making—still the most beautiful thing Cori had ever heard.

Afterward, lying together, Cori fell swiftly to sleep while

Aster ran her fingers across her back in that perfectly soothing way.

When she woke sometime later, with no concept of how much time had passed, Cori found Aster watching her.

"Hey, you," Aster said with a smile. "You slept hard."

"Did I?"

"Mhmm." Aster touched her cheek. "I hope it was as peaceful as it looked."

"Were you not sleeping?"

"I was, but I woke up three hours ago."

"Oh, shit, what time—"

"Close to midday. Since this is your day off, I decided not to wake you."

"Ah," Cori said, getting reoriented. "I don't usually sleep that long."

"I know."

Cori climbed out of bed to freshen up and returned to find Aster sitting up and looking like she had something to say.

Cori sat beside her on the bed and slipped an arm around her waist.

"I was thinking," Aster said, "about where to go next. I know we haven't talked about it yet, but I really need to go home—back to Centauride. I haven't seen my mothers since way before all this started. So maybe we could go there for now, and then... figure out what's next?"

"Aster! I *love* that idea!"

"You do?" she asked, visibly relieved.

"Of course! I can't wait to see it—and to meet them. Why the hesitation?"

"I don't know! I wasn't sure what you'd think about a spontaneous vacation."

Cori gave her a look. "I'd say we've both earned it."

Aster smiled and hugged her, pressing a kiss to her cheek. "Also, you should know . . . my mothers are wonderful, but they can be *a lot*."

"I don't know what that means, but I'm looking forward to finding out."

Aster laughed out loud, but then her smile fell a bit. "I just mean . . . there will probably be a lot of big emotions. Positive and negative. Since I've been away so long."

Cori nodded and rubbed her back. "That makes sense."

Aster leaned into her, and Cori held her. After a moment, Cori gave her a little wiggle.

"What was that for?" Aster asked, laughing again.

"I'm *so* excited!"

17

Centauride

Twenty-four years ago

Aster was five years old, home from school for the day and feeling restless. She wandered onto the back porch of her apartment and walked out to the railing to look down at the little park below.

Something caught her eye: a purple flower peeking down from the neighbor's porch above. If she could reach it, she could give it to Mommy Mona later when she got home—she *loved* purple. But it was too high.

Looking around, Aster spotted the trellis off to the side, where Mommy Cass grew her vines, and quickly discovered that her bare feet fit easily into the gaps. Climbing it like a ladder, she moved slowly upward, feeling the planks wobble under her weight. From up there, she had an even better view of the park—she had never seen so much of it from above. Refocusing on the flower, she still wasn't close enough to reach it, so she took another step, putting her fully above the railing.

Then two hands grasped under her armpits from behind, so firm that it hurt, and hauled her away from the trellis.

"No!" she cried, reaching for the flower in vain.

"WHAT are you *THINKING*?" Mommy Cass shouted. "Do you want to fall over the edge and go splat on the ground? Huh? Use your HEAD, kid!"

Aster couldn't respond, couldn't look at her. Mommy Cass didn't usually yell like that. Hot tears blurred her vision as she hurried back inside and ran to Mommy Mona's art room. She wasn't home yet, but Aster wished she were there, standing quietly looking at her paintings and crying.

"Aster?" came another voice—it was Mommy Kaitlyn this time. "Is that you? There you are! What's wrong, sweetie?"

"Nothing," she mumbled, wiping her eyes.

Kaitlyn bent down to be on her level and touched her shoulder. She always smelled nice.

"Are you okay?" she asked, running a hand over Aster's hair. "Hmm?"

"I . . . I want Mommy Mona to come home."

"Aww—me, too. We'll see her soon. What if I read to you while we wait? Yeah?"

They sat on the couch together. Kaitlyn read one of Aster's favorite stories, about a little girl with a pet bird, which was an animal that lived on planets and could fly. There was no such thing as a bird on Centauride, except in pictures and videos, but one day Aster would go to a planet and see one for real.

After some time, Mommy Mona came through the door, setting down her bag of art supplies. Aster leapt off the couch and ran to her. "Mama!"

Mona gave her a big smile and dropped to her knees to hug her, like she always did. "Aster! How's my sweet girl?"

She straightened up, and Aster leaned into her. She wasn't paying attention to what Mona was saying to Kaitlyn, nor did she notice when Cass came in—until Cass spoke to her.

"Is this what you were after?" she asked, poking her shoulder. Aster turned and saw that Cass was holding the purple flower. "When I saw you *climbing up the trellis?*"

Mona gasped. "Aster!"

She hid her face against the soft fabric of Mona's flowy pants.

"I'm sorry for yelling, sweetie," Cass went on. "But that was very dangerous, and you *can't* do that. If you fell off, your Mommy Mona would come home and push *me* off the porch, too."

"Cass, you *yelled* at her?" she heard Kaitlyn say. "No wonder she was so upset."

"I did say sorry, but you should have seen . . ."

Mona was guiding Aster away, so the other two voices

got quieter. She sat down in a soft chair in the next room, easing Aster into her lap.

"This is a pretty flower," Mona said.

Aster looked at it in surprise, not having realized she had it.

"Do you know what it's called?"

Aster shook her head.

"It's an aster. Just like your name."

Aster looked up at her face. "But I thought aster means *star*?"

"It does, that's right. I guess whoever named it thought this flower looked a little bit like a star, too."

Aster smiled, looking back at the flower. "I wanted to give it to you."

"Well, I love it. But do you understand why Mommy Cass said you can't climb there? If you fell off, you would get hurt. That would be terrible. All your mommies would be sad if that happened."

Aster nodded. "I know."

She kissed her cheek. "I missed you."

"Me, too. Mama?"

"Yes, lovely?"

"Would you *really* push Mommy Cass off the porch?"

She laughed. "No! I would never, ever do that. She meant that I'd be angry with her if you got hurt because she wasn't watching you. She was scared that something bad might happen when she saw you there. She loves you. That's why she got the flower for you."

Aster reached out for it, and Mona let her hold it. It was neat to see up close, with thin petals and a bright yellow center.

"We're the luckiest mommies ever, you know? Because we get to have you."

Aster squirmed at that and looked down at her lap. They went into the den for supper; she found that Cass was making one of her favorite stews.

Mona kept the flower in a little vase at first, and when it began to wilt, she took it and showed Aster how to press it flat and put it into a frame, which she hung on her studio wall.

✳ ✳ ✳

Present

Cori could tell Aster was anxious about returning to Centauride, although she didn't understand why. It seemed like the long-overdue visit should be a source of relief and joy, yet Aster was fidgety and quiet. Rather than asking any questions, Cori just held her hand, hoping her presence offered some comfort.

During the journey, Aster had told her a little about each of her mothers, which made Cori more excited to meet them. They also discussed how to handle the story of how they met, since Aster didn't want to burden her mothers with the truth of her previous circumstances. Cori had expected that plan to put Aster more at ease, but she had lost count of the times Aster had taken deep, nervous breaths. Family stuff was complicated, Cori gleaned.

When they exited the transit docks and stepped into the station, though, Cori briefly forgot any other concerns. Because she was standing in the most beautiful place she had ever seen.

It was nothing like Victory or its opposite, Ascension—Centauride was a calming oasis by comparison, with wide pathways, gleaming metal structures, colorful windows, and *plants*. Everywhere, plants. Lining the bridges, hanging over balconies, climbing up poles. The place looked—and smelled—like one massive greenhouse.

"Aster," Cori remarked in awe, "this is amazing."

Aster nodded. "This is home. I missed that smell."

As they made their way onward, Cori was too stunned to say anything more—captivated by the scenery. She thought back to Aster's fondness for the agriculture level on Victory. Of course she was drawn to it when *this* was her home.

✳ ✳ ✳

After dropping off their bags at their hotel, they continued on to Aster's childhood home: a corner apartment with a cozy porch where a woman with braided gray hair and work boots was tending to some flower boxes. As they approached, she turned to look at them and smiled.

"Hey, kid!" she said, standing and wiping her hands on her pants.

"Hi, Mom," Aster responded, bending down a bit to hug her.

This had to be Cass, Cori knew—the one who liked cooking and gardening.

"Nice to meet you," Cori said.

"There's an accent I don't hear every day," Cass remarked, taking Cori's hand in a firm grasp. "Glad you both made it."

"Glad to be here!"

Cass turned her attention back to Aster, playfully smacking her arm. "You look good! Are you good?"

Aster nodded. "I'm really good, now."

"They're both in here," Cass said, holding the door open for them.

"Thank you," Cori said, stepping inside.

The next person they saw was a woman with long dark hair and a colorful robe accented by several beaded necklaces: Kaitlyn.

"Hi, Mom," Aster said as they hugged.

"Hi, sweetheart. We've been *very* worried about you."

"I know."

"Kaity, don't be negative, dear," came another voice.

Cori turned to find a woman who bore such a striking

resemblance to Aster that she couldn't look away. She was slightly shorter, her face a bit thinner and lined with age, but the delicate point of her nose and her light eyes were nearly an exact match, as was her red hair—streaked with gray and twisted into a bun.

"Hi, Mom," Aster said for the third time, stepping quickly toward her and pulling her into her arms a bit more urgently than the first two.

"I wasn't being negative," Kaitlyn whispered to Cass, who wrapped an arm around her.

"I know," Aster said in reply, looking at all three of them. "I know I had you all worried. I'm really sorry I couldn't get back sooner."

"We're just glad you're alright, lovely," Mona said, touching Aster's braid. "Let me look at you. Your hair is so long! And my stars—your arm!"

"Yeah, it's getting crowded!" She held it out, and the other two stepped closer to look at her collection of tattoos.

Cass whistled. "Mona, how in the 'verse did you give birth to an *explorer*?"

Mona chuckled lightly. "They're beautiful, dear."

"Oh," Aster said, turning toward Cori for the first time since they'd come inside. "Sorry—this is Cori, my partner."

A second round of hellos followed, and then the question they anticipated.

"How did the two of you meet?" Kaitlyn asked.

"She's a doctor, and I went in with tendonitis in my elbow," Aster said quickly. "We clicked."

"We certainly did," Cori agreed. "She recommended a book, and it was already one of my favorites."

"A doctor," Cass said, sounding surprised. "Do you know that you're the first person she's *ever* brought home to meet us?"

Cori laughed. "I didn't know, but I'm honored. And I'm very happy to meet you all."

"Where does your family live?" Mona asked.

"Oh, I don't have one," Cori said. "I grew up in a military school on Earth."

All three of them looked stunned.

"My stars," Mona said softly.

"You were one of the ones they rescued," Kaitlyn said in apparent awe.

"That's right," Cori confirmed. "When I was seventeen."

Cass came over to her and clapped her on the shoulder. "Well, you have a family now, honey! Better get used to it."

Cori laughed again. "How kind of you!"

Aster shook her head, rubbing a hand over her face.

✳ ✳ ✳

They sat in the living room and drank fresh tea as they caught up. Aster's mothers seemed to be in high spirits, though there were a couple questions about her "shipping job," which Aster answered with what Cori recognized as careful lies inspired by the premise of *Asterism Entangled*: They'd met nearly a year ago (at least that part was true), since Cori worked at a station on Aster's route, and thereafter saw each other regularly when Aster had layovers there. Cori nodded along as Aster spoke, as if Aster were describing fond shared memories.

When her mothers moved on from that topic and started recapping things she missed while she was away, Aster relaxed a bit more.

The family dynamic was fascinating, but through all of it, Cori couldn't stop looking back at Mona, in awe of the resemblance. Eventually, Mona noticed, meeting Cori's gaze and smiling.

"Do you want to ask me something, dear?"

"Oh, no," Cori said, laughing. "I apologize for staring. It's just ... you look so much alike."

Everyone chuckled.

"Yeah, little Aster looked like a mini-Mona," Cass quipped.

"I imagine so!" Cori said.

Mona smiled at Cori again. "Come with me. Let me show you something."

Cori followed her into the hallway, leaving the other two to continue catching up with Aster. Mona led her into a room that turned out to be an art studio. There were stacks of paintings propped against the walls, flanked by shelves full of supplies. It was only when Mona gestured to a wall of framed photos that Cori understood the reason for bringing her here.

Aster was in nearly every picture. There was a shot of her as a child in Mona's lap, both of them with matching red hair clipped up on one side. There was another of them in Aster's adolescence, Cori guessed, when she had surpassed Mona in height—Aster was leaning into her mother and scrunching up her face in an exaggerated grin. In yet another, she was somewhere in between those ages and proudly holding up her own artwork. There was a smaller one off to the side, where Aster was unrecognizable: a sleeping baby swaddled in a blanket.

Cori's vision swam. For one thing, it was incredible to see memories from Aster's early life—her happy childhood, unlike anything Cori ever knew. For another, Cori couldn't help but see the beautiful moments through Mona's eyes, understanding more deeply than before how much she must have ached for her daughter to return.

"Mona, these are amazing. Thank you for sharing them with me."

"Oh, goodness, are you alright?" she asked, rubbing Cori's back in a familiar way.

"Yes," she said, unconvincingly. "I've just never seen anything like . . . I never realized—I never—"

Mona pulled her into a gentle hug, which she returned.

"Thank you for helping my baby," Mona said softly, "and bringing her home."

"She's the best person I've ever met."

From the doorway behind her, Cori heard Aster's voice.

"Are you in— Oh. Yeah, that figures."

They both turned to look at her.

"Are you *both* crying?"

The embrace became a group hug as Aster threw her arms around them.

"Let me give the two of you some space," Cori said as they moved apart. "I'm sure you have a lot to talk about."

Aster touched her shoulder as she left the room. Cori headed back to the lounge area, only to find Cass and Kaitlyn kissing on the sofa.

"Oh," she said under her breath, starting another direction.

"Hey, come back," Cass said.

"Sorry, didn't mean to interrupt."

"You're not," Kaitlyn said with a smile, adjusting her robe.

"Mona was showing me some wonderful photos," Cori explained as she dropped to a chair.

"Ah, yes, her collage," Kaitlyn said fondly.

"Photos?" Cass echoed. "You want to see *more*? We've got more!"

"I'd love to!"

WHERE STARLIGHT BURNS

✻ ✻ ✻

Aster and her mother passed through the apartment and onto the back porch. Mona had been unusually quiet, like maybe she was afraid of what she'd say if she spoke too much.

"Ah," Aster said, looking down at the park below. "I missed this view."

It took Mona a moment to respond. When she did, her voice was small and sad. "I was getting worried that you weren't coming back."

"It wasn't that I didn't want to," Aster said, facing her. "It was never that. I just . . . got involved with the wrong people. I had some financial trouble for a while. I had to fix it. I couldn't come home until it was all sorted out."

Mona looked at her with sorrowful eyes, brow furrowed. "It wasn't just *tendonitis*, was it?"

Aster blinked. She hadn't expected Mona to see right through that.

"Not just. But that did happen."

"Hmm. I don't want to know, do I?"

Aster shook her head, eyes prickling. "I'm *really* sorry, Mom. I never meant to be away that long. I never meant to worry you so much."

With the same sadness in her eyes, Mona stepped forward and hugged her. Aster returned the embrace gently, finding for the second time that Mona felt thinner than she remembered.

"I'm so glad you're alright," she said. "And Cori seems very sweet."

"She's the best. Like, genuinely the best. I know you'll think so, too, when you get to know her."

"I already do," she said with a sincere smile. "I'm glad you found each other."

"Me, too. And honestly . . . if things hadn't happened the way they did, I never would have met her. I feel like I'm lucky just to *know* her."

"Goodness," Mona said with a chuckle. "I've never heard you talk that way about anyone. You must really love her."

Aster nodded. "I want to marry her. And we're going to stay here for a while, on Centauride."

Mona smiled again and squeezed her arm. "Until a new adventure calls, I'm sure."

There was a faint chiming sound somewhere inside.

"Ohh," Mona groaned, as though she had remembered something irritating.

Before Aster could ask, Kaitlyn appeared in the doorway.

"Mo," she said, holding up a small package.

"Right *now*?" Mona asked.

Kaitlyn gave her a look. "It'll only take a second. You'll be in pain again if we skip."

"What is it?" Aster asked, looking between them.

"Patches for her wrist pain," Kaitlyn said.

"Wrist pain?" Aster asked, looking back at Mona.

WHERE STARLIGHT BURNS

"Fine, come on then," Mona said to Kaitlyn, and they both moved to a cushioned bench on the porch.

Aster watched as Kaitlyn gently peeled two thin patches from each of Mona's wrists and replaced them with new ones, taking great care to get the placement right. It was no wonder Mona couldn't do it herself—it required two hands.

"Does that feel okay?" Kaitlyn asked, touching her shoulder.

"Yes, thank you, sweetie."

"Good. Sorry to interrupt."

"No, Kaity," Mona said, reaching out for her and pressing a kiss to her cheek. "You're always taking good care of me. Even when I'm stubborn."

"How long have you had wrist pain?" Aster asked.

"Off and on for about a year now," Mona said. "From painting."

"And it gets worse with stress," Kaitlyn added, ignoring the look Mona gave her.

"A year? They couldn't heal it for you?"

Mona shook her head. "The doctor said the inflammation was too small for the lamps, so I have to wait for it to get worse before they can do that."

"Hmm," Aster said. "That seems odd. Maybe Cori can take a look—I'll ask her."

She stepped back inside just far enough to poke her head into the hallway and call her name. Cori appeared a moment later, and Aster led her to the porch, explaining what she'd heard.

"Does that sound right?" Aster asked as they stepped onto the porch together.

"Without seeing her scans, I can't be sure," Cori said, stepping closer to Mona. "Where on your wrists is it, if you don't mind showing me?"

She pointed to the fresh patch. "Just here."

"I see. I can understand their reasoning in theory, since it might be better to use the patches as a temporary fix, but if nothing changed in a year, I'd want to be more proactive."

"We have her most recent scans, if that would help," Kaitlyn said.

Cori directed her attention to Mona. "Would that be alright with you?"

"Sure," she said. "In fact, let me get my comm—it'll be easier that way."

Cori followed Mona back into the house, leaving Aster alone on the porch with Kaitlyn. Kaitlyn regarded her coolly for a moment, which didn't surprise her. Kaitlyn was the least enthusiastic about her decision to travel so much.

"Is it worse than she said?" Aster asked.

Kaitlyn shrugged. "Good days and bad. *You* had her worried half to death."

"I know...I understand if you're angry with me."

"No, you don't," she said, shaking her head. "You can't. Because you weren't here."

"I did come back as soon as I could."

Kaitlyn gave her a sad look and started to pace. "When you're here, she *glows*. You don't see what happens when that glow fades. I watched her become a shell of herself missing you. I stayed up nights with her when she couldn't sleep because she was *so* afraid that she'd never see you again. We were *all* afraid of that."

She paused to wipe her eyes. Aster did the same, at a loss for words. Kaitlyn was always protective—of her, when she was young, and of Mona, which Aster didn't fully understand until she grew older. Now, her words hit with the benefit of lived experience: Kaitlyn's partner was heartbroken, and she was powerless to fix it.

"I'm sorry, Mom," she said. "I never meant to cause so much pain. I'm *really* glad she has you."

Kaitlyn blinked, frowning. Before she could respond, Mona shouted from the doorway.

"Kaity! *What* were you just telling her out here?"

"Only the truth."

Mona looked at Aster, then, and she knew her face must have been a mess. Mona snapped back to Kaitlyn, jabbing the air with her finger. "What did I tell you about being *negative*!"

"She's a grown adult, Mo. She can handle it."

"She *just* got back!" Mona scolded, voice wavering. "Do you want to . . . push her away?"

"That's not going to happen," Aster said firmly. "I *want* to be here. And Mom . . . Kaitlyn is right."

She wasn't sure which one of them looked more shocked by that statement.

"She was just being honest with me. I'm really sorry for everything I put you through."

"Aster," Mona said, composing herself, "you don't need to keep apologizing to us. You came home. That's what matters. That's all we wanted."

She hugged Aster again. In the silence that followed, Kaitlyn stepped back inside without a word. Aster belatedly realized that Cori had been standing there with them, too, when she followed Kaitlyn, giving Aster a nod as she left the porch.

"Mom, don't be mad at her, okay? I know you're both just frustrated with *me*."

Mona gave her a sad smile. "When did you get so wise?"

Aster laughed. "I have my moments. Did Cori figure anything out with your scans?"

"Not exactly; she said she can take new ones and see what the options are. Very kind of her."

"I'm sure she's happy to do it."

A silent moment passed while Mona glanced at nothing in particular.

"There are certain things you shouldn't have to know," she said after a while. "Just like there are things you aren't going to tell me, which I respect. I didn't want her to burden you with that."

"I'm sure there are lots of things I still don't know," Aster offered. "She didn't tell me anything that shocked me."

"I love you," Mona said, rubbing her arm. "I missed you. I'm very proud of you. I always have been."

"Love you, too."

✷ ✷ ✷

In the kitchen, Cori was sitting on a counter stool and watching as Cass warmed a soup for supper. Cass filled the silence with ease, talking about how Aster used to sit in the same spot while she cooked and ask a hundred questions about what she was doing.

After a while, Aster and Mona returned.

"That smells good," Aster said.

"Where—" Mona started.

Cass gave her a look and pointed down the hall, toward the room where Kaitlyn had quickly disappeared after the heated porch discussion. Mona turned to go that way.

Aster took the seat beside Cori, looking worried, like she might say something. Before she did, though, Cass handed her a sample of the soup in a small cup.

"How's that?" she asked with a twinkle in her eye.

"Mmm," she said after a taste, her concern melting into happiness. "Delicious as always."

"Good. Are you two ready to eat?"

"Should we not wait for—" Aster started, but Cass waved her off.

"They'll be in here any minute. They're fine."

Cori and Aster gladly accepted full bowls and warm bread, moving to the table to eat and converse with Cass. Unlike her wives, she behaved like this was any other dinner, relaxed and witty at every turn. It was very interesting, Cori found, to observe Aster's unique relationship with each of her mothers.

Mona and Kaitlyn re-emerged shortly, quietly serving themselves and joining the others at the table. The earlier tension seemed to evaporate as they entered the conversation. Cori was once again fascinated by the family dynamic—there was a *fourth* relationship, she realized, when all of them were together.

As they talked, Cori thought about how long Aster had gone without this connection, without this sharing, and how a piece of her heart must have always been tugging at her to return here.

✳ ✳ ✳

After they said their goodbyes and started the walk back to their hotel room for the evening, Aster felt ready to collapse. Cori must have been able to tell because she didn't say anything until after they were back inside.

"How are you?" she asked.

Aster shrugged. "Exhausted."

"It *has* been a long day."

"How are *you*? I know that was a lot."

Cori sighed in a long, drawn-out way that was uncharacteristic of her.

"Hey," Aster said, slipping her arms around her. "What is it?"

Cori took a moment longer to respond. When she did, her voice was small and soft. "I've never been anchored to anyone. I heard people talk about their families, of course, and I thought I understood, but . . ." She paused to shake her head. "You must have missed them *so* much, all the time, and I never knew."

"To be fair, I didn't mention it," Aster said. "Talking about them made the guilt too heavy. But I'm really glad we're here now."

Cori pressed a kiss to her cheek. "Me, too."

They embraced, then, and didn't let go for a while.

"Aster," Cori said with new conviction in her voice, "I think we should live here. I think Centauride could be our home."

Aster laughed in surprise. "I haven't even given you the tour yet."

"I'm looking forward to it. But I think I've seen what matters."

Aster wasn't sure how to respond. Part of her wanted to

be overjoyed, but another part didn't want to rush Cori into this. "But we're not even sure if the clinic—"

"We'll make it work," Cori said with clear certainty.

"You *really* want to live here."

"I do. If you like the idea."

"I definitely do. But maybe we should both sleep on it?"

Cori smiled. "I think sleeping is a good idea."

18

Vows

Twenty years ago — Earth

Corinth-N deposited her meal cup into the cleaning receptacle in the mess hall, behind Corinth-M and before Corinth-O, like she did every morning. Most days, it would be time for warm-ups now, before training exercises, but instead, it was the day she secretly liked best: their weekly history lesson.

Corinth-N enjoyed history because she liked imagining a time when the planet looked different. The old texts described a lively, bountiful place, with enormous landmasses covered with green plants and people living in homes. Sometimes, it was hard to believe that it was really like that at all. Maybe it was just a story they told children. But, no, she felt it must be true, for some reason she couldn't explain.

They lined up by the exit just as the Sydney squad came

inside, drenched from a morning jog in the rain. At fifteen, they were five years older than the Corinths, fully grown and towering over them as they passed by.

Outside, the Corinths crossed the main bridge from the barracks over to the education building. It was drizzling now, a few acidic raindrops running down Corinth-N's smooth head and stinging her eyes, while a whisper of sunlight glowed through the gray haze of the sky. Below the bridge, the seemingly endless expanse of murky brown ocean churned and gurgled. Corinth-N always looked down at the waves, hoping to catch sight of a shiny fish...or something even more special. One of her favorite stories from the old world was about a *mermaid*—a girl with beautiful red hair and a fish tail instead of legs—who lived deep in the ocean, in a secret underwater palace. Corinth-N never told anyone, but she hoped that if she looked every time, she might someday see a *real* mermaid, and maybe the mermaid would notice her, too. Maybe they could be friends. Maybe Corinth-N could go with her to the mermaid palace and live there instead of doing training and drills.

"Triumph! Humanity! Tradition!" the group chanted as they passed under the Earth emblem at the entrance to the school. They went down the hall to the archive, with its computers and databases and *books*. Corinth-N would never forget the first time they toured the library: the tall shelves, the smell of the pages, and the ink used to mark the words on the brown paper. *Relics*, they were called, those remnants of their ancestors' lives. *We must be very careful with them.*

While the rest of the group took their seats in the main lecture hall, she tried her luck, making an excuse to slip down a nearby hallway and around a corner, where she could peer through the window of a locked door and see the bookshelves from afar. She would pretend she was only in the lavatory, as she always did, when she returned a moment later. But first, she had to see them. It was nice to know they were still there.

Just as she was about to start back, though, the lights shifted to red, and an alarm sounded. *Not a drill,* she thought in frustration. *Not today.*

But then she heard adults nearby shouting, scrambling. They weren't expecting this. She felt a pit in her stomach at the thought that this could be a real attack.

There came a loud boom, and then another, and everything went dark.

When Corinth-N woke up, she could hear muffled voices somewhere nearby. She couldn't move, though—something heavy was holding her down. She tried to shout only to cough instead, her throat dry with dust. That turned out to be enough to alert someone to her location, since they were swiftly hauling her upward.

"State your name," said an adult in combat armor—*Oslo-G*, she read on his helmet.

"Corinth-N," she managed, hoarsely.

"N. Well, you're the lucky one. Are you injured?"

"No," she said, since the only pain she felt was a dull headache.

Oslo-G set her down in a clear spot. Looking around, Corinth-N realized that the archive—and half of the school—had been reduced to rubble. The lecture hall was gone, and on the ground before her were the bodies of the other Corinths, with burns marring their identical faces. If they'd been old enough to have undergone the cybernetic enhancement procedures, they might have survived.

In a moment of sudden terror, she turned to look at where the library used to be and saw nothing but ash and metal.

"The books," she said out loud without really meaning to. "Where are the books?"

"Save your anger for Mars," was the only answer she got.

Mars, of course, did this, Corinth-N knew. They didn't care about history or tradition or anything special from the past. They only wanted to destroy. And that's why Earth would defeat them.

***

Present

Cori's eyes flashed open in the early hours of the morning, in the unfamiliar bedroom of their hotel on Centauride. It took her a moment to realize why she was awake, when she heard Aster whining in her sleep.

Turning to face her, Cori rubbed her arm. In the dim light, she could see that Aster's brow was furrowed. After a moment, Aster whimpered again, as if in pain.

"Aster?" Cori said, giving her shoulder a little wiggle.

Waking with a start, Aster sat up and hunched over, clutching her stomach.

"Breathe," Cori said, sitting up beside her. "You're okay. You're awake now."

Aster spoke between ragged breaths. "Fucking stars. That felt so real."

"What?" Cori asked, moving hair away from her face. "You can tell me."

"I felt something inside," Aster said softly, rubbing her hand over her stomach. "Moving, hurting. Exactly like... the parasite."

Cori gently rested her hand flat against Aster's stomach. "Nothing moving here. Do you still feel it?"

Aster shook her head, breathing more evenly now. "That was so weird. I've never dreamed about it before."

She leaned into Cori, and Cori gathered her up. "You're free now," Cori said after some time. "Which means you're also free to process what happened to you in a way you never were before. Don't be afraid of the dreams—or the memories. Just let yourself process it."

Aster shifted in her arms and pressed a kiss to Cori's jaw. "Do you still dream about Earth?"

"Oh, yes. Frequently. But the dreams don't affect my emotions. Not anymore. They're just . . . mental relics. Facts of my past that led me to where I am now."

Aster resettled into her arms, and they held each other until the daylight cycle began.

✳ ✳ ✳

Later that morning, the two of them set out early and stopped for breakfast at one of Aster's favorite cafes, popular for its traditional Centauride food and unique decor: the bushes were trimmed into odd shapes, and long vines on the walls spelled out words. It was highly surreal—in a good way—to be sitting there with Cori, who beamed all through the meal.

Next, they wandered through the zone where Aster grew up, with its towers of stacked residence units and pretty courtyards. As always, there were lots of families around, vendors selling pastries and crafts, and so many botanists, with their belts of supplies, thoroughly tending the plants on a regular rotation—some of them used hover chairs to float up to the greenery growing in spaces harder to access, which Aster had loved to watch as a child.

Cori was awed by it all, remarking over and over how cozy and welcoming the station was. Aster appreciated the validation; it was nice to know that it wasn't just her personal bias.

After getting stuck with her debt, when Aster had made peace with the fact that she wouldn't be able to return home for a while, she had sealed off the part of herself that would miss it. She knew she couldn't afford to be *homesick* on top of everything else—it would have been an unhelpful emotion. So, it wasn't until they were in a rail car, looking out at the sprawling heart of the hub, that it really started to sink in. She was finally back. She made it.

"Oh, wow!" Cori said beside her, admiring the view, unaware of Aster swallowing a lump in her throat.

Centauride *was* a visually striking place, with its metallic buildings and artistic accents, and the other rail trains like this one, winding through the verdure all around. Aster spent so much of her youth longing to see other places and little time appreciating this station. But maybe that had been the point of traveling all along—to come home and see it in a new context, through wiser eyes.

"There aren't aliens here, are there?" Cori asked, snapping Aster back to the present. "Just humans?"

"Just human residents, yeah, except for the very rare visitor. That's pretty common in this region of space—just like there are areas with almost no humans. It's one of the things that made me want to see other places when I was young. I felt like I was missing out."

Cori considered that for a moment. "In all your years

of traveling, did you see any other stations that were *this* beautiful?"

Aster smiled at that, cycling through a mental slideshow of her favorites. There was Valtiak, crisp and clean and modern, with its pretty cycle lighting, incredibly plush beds, and friendly people. There was Pegasus, with its wild, untamed vegetation, where edible plants were open for general consumption and festivals were common. And there was Epsilon IV, with questionable aesthetics but famously delicious cuisine, thanks to its orbit around an agriculture planet.

"I saw a lot of great places," Aster said after a moment. "A lot of unique and fun stations. But this one always feels like home. So it's hard for anything to compare to that."

"I know exactly what you mean, even though I just got here. Maybe it's contagious."

"Would you believe I found it *boring* when I was young?" Aster asked.

"Boring?! Well, I guess I *can* believe it. Since you were so adventurous... What about now?"

Aster blinked. "Now?"

"Do you still find it boring in some way?"

"Not really," Aster said, glancing out the window. "I appreciate it more than I did when I was young. I think I'm finally ready for familiar and comfortable."

Cori took her hand, lacing their fingers together.

"I *did* have a feeling you'd like it," Aster added.

"And you were right."

WHERE STARLIGHT BURNS

✳ ✳ ✳

The final stop of their tour was the station archive, which Aster was also confident Cori would enjoy. The building itself spanned two station floors and housed a database of all residents, plus an extensive library. Bordering the structure was the archive gardens, a lush area with paths winding through the colorful flowers and greenery. It was always one of Aster's favorite places to visit as a child. As an adult she was even more impressed—the grounds were perfectly maintained by the garden staff, and the plants always looked pristine.

"This is all so pretty!" Cori said as they passed through a tunnel covered in thick vines bearing yellow blooms.

Aster smiled; it was only about the twelfth time Cori had said so. At the other end of the tunnel, they wandered into a more secluded area with flowering trees. There weren't any other people around. It was the perfect spot. Aster grasped Cori's elbow, slowing them to a stop.

"Let's pause for a minute," she said, swallowing.

"Okay!" Cori said, turning to her and smiling.

Aster chuckled, feeling the tiniest hint of nerves. "You already know what I'm going to say."

"I have no ide— Oh!" Cori's big eyes went wider.

Aster laughed again and took both of her hands. "Well, now that I spoiled the surprise, I'll keep this short... From the first day we met, when I was lower than I'd ever been, you've made me feel safe. I could already tell you were someone I was lucky to cross paths with. Since then, by being with you, I've learned what love should really feel like. I don't know what I ever did to be lucky enough for *you* to love me back, but I thank the stars for bringing us together every day. And I'll keep doing that for the rest of my life. If you'll marry me."

"Aster." Cori blinked tears from her eyes. Without saying more, she pulled Aster into an urgent hug.

Aster returned the embrace, and they stood in silence for a while.

"Aster," Cori said again, composing herself. "I love you, and I'm grateful all the time, too, just to know you. It would be the greatest honor of my life to marry you."

They kissed, not caring that a few other people had wandered into that section of the garden.

"If you'd like to make it official now," Aster said, gesturing to the archive, "we happen to be in the right place."

Cori's face lit up. "Oh! But...you don't want a wedding?"

"Not unless you do," Aster said with a smile and a shrug. "I just want to be married to you."

Cori smiled at that, clearly on board. They went inside, up to the records floor where they could officially list each other as spouses—and as residents of Centauride.

When everything was confirmed in the system, Aster pulled her *wife* into a new embrace.

The archivist there offered to take a celebratory photo

of them on the balcony nearby, which they gladly accepted. Moments later, when Cori was looking at the picture on her comm, both of them smiling so big, and pretty Centauride in the background, she sighed with delight. "What a perfect day."

"I actually have one more small surprise," Aster said.

Cori looked adorably confused. "Really?"

"Just a few floors up."

"Well, lead the way!"

Aster took Cori up to a space she remembered from her school trips: the antique library, with walls bearing large shelves of paper books. As they stepped inside, Aster expected to hear some exclamation from Cori, some gasp of awe, and so when she was completely silent, Aster turned to see why. She found Cori stopped in her tracks and staring ahead with unblinking awe.

"Hey... are you okay?" Aster asked softly, moving closer to her and touching her shoulder.

"I've never seen so many in one room."

They stepped closer to get a better look. Cori marveled at some of the historic titles she recognized. The books weren't physically accessible to the public—only the spines were visible—but the library's sophisticated interface allowed anyone to zoom in on the shelves, virtually select a book, and flip through lifelike scans of its cover and pages.

Aster stood beside her at each shelf, arm around her waist, watching her *wife* have fun browsing in their shared feed. At the section for Earth history, Cori opened a few illustrated children's books, written in dead languages with translated captions. Cori didn't say anything about them out loud, but Aster got the sense that they were familiar.

"This was a beautiful surprise," Cori said, deeply sincere, after closing what might have been her fiftieth book.

"We can come back anytime you want."

"Yes, we can, can't we?" Cori said, slipping her arms around Aster's waist and kissing her. "Since this is our home now."

✳ ✳ ✳

Back in the privacy of their hotel room, Aster pulled Cori into a long hug. Cori eagerly returned the embrace, elated to think that Aster would be able to live a safe and healthy life now, and that they could begin a new chapter of their lives together on Centauride.

The embrace became a kiss. Without speaking, Cori knew from the way Aster lingered on her lips and held her waist that they would be in bed shortly. Not really meaning to, she thought back to the beginning of their relationship and how she'd been unsure what to expect when it came to intimacy. Now, there were no more mysteries. It was almost surreal to think that making love with this incredible, gorgeous person had become so comfortable and common in a way Cori never would have dared to dream.

Above her in bed, Cori could see similar sentiments written on Aster's face. It was their first time doing this as spouses, of course. Cori pressed kisses to each of Aster's flushed cheeks before trailing down to her jaw and neck and torso—and then lower still, relishing the way Aster purred a bit more urgently with the descent.

The sheets on the bed were pale green, and Aster's hair stood in pretty contrast as she lay looking up at Cori, adoring and serene. Cori couldn't do anything other than stare for a moment. She had been struck by Aster's beauty since the first time they met, but now Aster was simply radiant.

Cori leaned down and kissed her again, wholly powerless to do anything else.

Moments later, Cori moved to lie beside her wife, running her fingers up Aster's thigh in the way she knew would make her eyes flutter shut. Cori pressed a kiss to her jaw, breathing the scent of Aster's hair—and the subtle, permeating aroma of Centauride's greenery—as her hand fell into what had become a natural rhythm.

Aster shifted to face her, then, touching her in the same way, and they wordlessly achieved a harmony together, alternating the ebb and surge. Perhaps sex would never stop being surreal on some level, not even when they had been married for ten or twenty years, but being *comfortable* together certainly improved it.

"I *love* you," Cori breathed, finding the words crucially important yet somehow insufficient.

Panting, Aster kissed her. "I love you, too."

They reached their peaks a second apart, crying out and laughing and then collapsing into each other.

Lying there and catching their breaths afterward, Aster hummed. "I guess we need to find an actual apartment soon."

"Yeah," Cori agreed, shifting to face her. "And...oh! We should go see your mothers and tell them the good news! All of it!"

Aster cringed. "Okay, yes, but I'm going to need more space between us having sex and you mentioning my *parents*."

Cori cupped a hand over her mouth. "Sorry."

"That's okay. Come here."

Cori was happily gathered into her arms, and they shared another kiss in the soft nest of the hotel bed.

19
Home

Just as the evening cycle was starting on Centauride, Aster made her way to her mothers' apartment, with her now-wife in tow. In contrast to the apprehension she felt the day before, she was buzzing with happy excitement to arrive with good news. Her mothers' individual reactions could be unpredictable, but *this* felt like a pretty safe bet.

"Aster! Cori!" Mona said, pulling each of them into hugs. "How was the tour?"

"I think it went pretty well," Aster said with a casual shrug, looking at Cori.

Cori laughed. "It was *wonderful*. All of it. But especially the end."

Cass and Kaitlyn came into the room behind Mona, looking curious.

"We visited the archive," Aster said, drawing it out, "annnnd officially registered as spouses."

There was a chorus of happy gasping.

"Aw, how wonderful!" Mona said.

"Hey, welcome to the family!" Cass said. "Now you're really stuck with us."

"Congratulations," Kaitlyn added. "Will there be a wedding?"

"Oh no," Aster said. "Not for now, at least. We just want to settle in."

"There *is* one other thing," Cori said, looking at Aster, "if it's alright to say?"

Aster nodded.

"We've decided to live on Centauride—permanently," Cori said.

That got them a stunned silence.

"Really?" Mona asked.

"Really," Aster said, meeting each skeptical glance. "I'm ready now. I've got my person. And luckily for me, she loves it here."

"I do!" Cori confirmed. "I'm so excited to call this station my new home."

"Well, that's *wonderful!*" Kaitlyn said, stepping forward and embracing each of them. "Mona, isn't that so wonderful?"

Mona smiled belatedly. "Of course it is! We'll be so happy to have you here."

Something about the way she said it seemed off, like

maybe she didn't believe it yet. That was understandable, given Aster's track record.

"I'd say this calls for a celebration," Cass chimed in.

"Absolutely!" Kaitlyn agreed. "We should all go out to dinner."

"I was thinking shots, but yeah, let's get fancy!"

They agreed to go to Hylonome's Table, a pretty restaurant in the arts district, one zone over. It was a place Aster remembered from several other special occasions—and one she could inwardly admit to having missed.

On the train ride there, she ended up next to Mona, while the other three were occupied with something Cass was pointing out through the window.

"So, you're sure about this?" Mona asked. "That you want to live here?"

"Yeah. Why wouldn't I be?"

"You just got back, is my point. Seems a bit sudden. For such a big decision."

Aster wasn't sure how to respond.

"Don't get me wrong," Mona added quickly. "It would make me *very* happy. But I just... Well, I would never want you to feel like you had to give up your adventures. Especially not because of us."

"I don't feel that way," Aster said, belatedly understanding her skepticism. "I got all that out of my system, honestly. I'm ready to settle down, to be home. Now that we're here, we both want to stay. I mean it."

Alicia Haberski

Mona smiled at that, her nose and eyelids flushed. "Good." After a beat, she pulled Aster into a new hug with some urgency. "That's so wonderful, my lovely."

✷ ✷ ✷

Hylonome's Table had a charming, cozy setup across multiple floors, and they ended up on the second story near a color-stained window. As Aster took her seat, she was struck for a moment by how *normal* the situation felt. Just sitting down to a meal with her family on her home station. Nothing specific or significant to worry about on the horizon. If it weren't for Cori sitting beside her, it might feel like the last few years were all a bizarre dream.

When they had settled in with their drinks, waiting for the food to arrive, the conversation focused on Cori—Aster's mothers were curious about her past, and she was happy to share, as always.

"Idun was a beautiful place," she said, "though the winters were rough where I lived. But after I finished my residency, I was ready to move on and see what life in space was like."

"Do you miss it at all?" Kaitlyn asked. "'Living on planets?"

"I don't know if I miss it," Cori responded. "Certain aspects of it, maybe . . . On Idun, the rain always had such a delicate, pleasant smell. You could smell the rain before it started, and then it would linger after it ended and the sun came out. That never got old."

"Well, we're very glad you decided to venture out," Mona said.

Cass and Kaitlyn voiced their agreement.

"So am I," Cori said, beaming. "I think deciding to relocate to a station was the best decision I ever made." She reached over to pat Aster's shoulder.

"Now that you've decided to live here, will you take up practice at a clinic?" Mona asked.

"Yes—hopefully. That's the plan. If I can find an opening sometime soon, in a clinic or lab to start with, maybe."

"What about you, Aster?" Cass asked from the end of the table. "What do *you* think you'll do here for work?"

It was an innocent question, but it made Aster's chest go tight; she wasn't really sure why. The concept of trying to decide on a job that actually *interested* her was a weirdly daunting prospect after what she endured the last few years. But she couldn't exactly explain any of that out loud.

"Uhhh," she blurted. "I'm not sure yet, but I'll . . . find something."

"All those odd jobs while you were station-hopping and *nothing* stood out?" Cass asked with a smirk, oblivious to her discomfort.

"I— I don't—" Aster stammered. Why the fuck were her hands shaking?

Cori took hold of her hand and squeezed tight. "You

have plenty of time to decide," she said, speaking in a slow, measured way. "There's absolutely no rush for you to start working."

For a moment, Aster just held her gaze and squeezed back, nodding.

"Something to think about," she said, facing her mothers again and forcing a smile.

Before anyone could ask more questions, the food arrived. Aster thought she caught Mona giving her a sad look just before her plate was set in front of her, but she looked away. Her own dish was twice-baked radish casserole, a Centauride staple, and the aroma evoked comfort and memories of childhood.

As she ate, she avoided looking at anyone else at the table, but the emotions got the best of her. A few tears fell into her food.

Cori set her fork down and touched Aster's shoulder, wordlessly rubbing.

"I'm fine," Aster said, cursing her eyes. "This is just so delicious. I missed it."

By the time they were finished with dinner, everyone was in good spirits, and Cass whispered something to the server—who returned with a cake to celebrate their marriage, frosted with cream and decorated with fruits and flowers. Cori reacted with excitement, and Aster gave Cass a look of gratitude. She winked.

As they enjoyed the dessert, Aster was very glad that

they'd already decided to stay. For the first time in a long while, she felt like she was in the *right* place.

✸ ✸ ✸

In all of Cori's life, she had never once personally selected an apartment. On Earth, she never had a space to call her own. Then, at the university and medical school, there was simply the campus housing assignment each year for her cohort—a small room just for her, with a bed and a desk and a window, often with a view of trees or a courtyard—which had felt like something out of a dream. On Victory and Ascension, she had taken the first apartment offered to her as a member of the medical staff.

So, now that she and Aster had *three* apartments to decide between on Centauride, she felt a little overwhelmed. But after two nights in the hotel, she was definitely in favor of making a choice soon.

"I mean it," she said, "I'll be happy in *any* of them!"

"I know you will. But I just wondered if you had a *preference*. And before you say no, think about it. Imagine living in each one we saw. There's the one that's more central, near the archive, but it's a bit small. There's the one closer to my moms' place, but it didn't have much of a view, in my opinion. And there's the third, the bigger one, which . . . well, it might be too big, honestly."

"That one's off the list, then!"

"Okay. So, between the first two?"

Cori took a breath. "Living within walking distance of your mothers might be nice—and you liked the kitchen there. But I do see what you mean about the view at the other place, and it had that neat little courtyard just downstairs."

Aster laughed and shook her head.

"I know! I'm not helping at all. But like I told you, I've never done this before, and it really can't be up to me. It's too much pressure! If you told me we were taking a spare room at your parents' place, I wouldn't argue!"

Aster looked mildly horrified. "Well, let's never imagine *that* again. In fact . . . maybe we take a break from thinking about this for now. We could go out for a walk and find some dinner? We don't have to decide immediately."

Cori was happy to agree. The evening cycle on Centauride was nothing short of magical, with day lighting dimmed to a whisper and hundreds of little algae lamps, some among the plants or perched atop posts, giving it a charming, romantic vibe as they walked hand in hand.

After three nice days on the station, Cori was no less excited about calling it home, but part of her wished they could skip ahead to a time when they would be settled in and everything was sorted out. To a time when she would be successfully employed—she had submitted her availability to both main clinics here—and Aster had found something she enjoyed doing, profitable or not.

Though Cori knew she shouldn't take this "vacation"

for granted, the transition period made her impatient for the future.

She realized Aster had paused and moved over to the edge of an overpass to examine the greenery. Cori stepped up beside her, wondering what had distracted her. All she saw were pretty leaves illuminated by lamplight.

"They're all so healthy," Aster observed. "No spots or wilted leaves on any of them. Isn't that amazing?"

"It is. They're impressively well cared for."

Aster nodded, looking deep in thought. Cori put an arm around her while she ran her fingers across a smooth leaf. From where they were standing on the side of the bridge, the view of this area of the zone was breathtaking, with people milling about here and there, crossing other overpasses or mingling in the courtyards below, bordered by shops and restaurants. Somewhere nearby, there was live music—string instruments, Cori thought. It was incredible to see this place and remember that Aster grew up *right here*, that all of these wonderful sights felt inherently like home to her.

In all their conversations about finding an apartment, Aster never once asked about the possibility of living in the staff suites at the clinic like they had before—maybe because they had no way of knowing when that would be, or because she didn't *want* to live that way anymore. So, Cori hadn't brought it up, either. She would never, not in a million years, ask her sweet wife to set foot near a hospital again unless completely necessary. No, what Aster needed was security and comfort, both in abundance.

"Sorry," Aster said, suddenly snapping out of her daze. "My mind was wandering."

"I think we should live close to your family," Cori said abruptly. "In this zone that you know so well. At least to start out. If you like the idea."

Aster smiled at that, raising her eyebrows. "I do. But what made up your mind?"

Cori shook her head. "Just you. Just a feeling."

Aster pulled her into a kiss beneath the lamps. They continued on, walking on winding paths through their pretty home. Cori felt deeply lucky to be here, in the most beautiful place she had ever seen, with her favorite person in the universe.

✳ ✳ ✳

While Cori was (finally) away for a round of introductions at the clinic, Aster visited her mothers and helped with a few things around their place. She was increasingly glad to have chosen the closer apartment and to be living in her old zone. Being somewhere so familiar was more refreshing—and healing—than she anticipated.

After midday, she ended up sprawled on the sofa, napping just like she used to do when she was younger. Only, this time, she dreamed of the parasite once again. The feeling of it twisting and moving in her gut was so specific, so vivid and real, that she woke with a start, sitting up and clutching her stomach before recalling where she actually was.

"Are you okay?"

Kaitlyn was standing in front of her, looking alarmed. She was the only other person here, at present.

Aster caught her breath. "Yeah, just a weird dream."

Kaitlyn didn't look convinced. "Want some cold water?"

"Sure. Thank you."

Kaitlyn stepped over to the kitchen and returned with a glass, taking a seat next to her, brows knit with concern. Aster swallowed a big sip, hoping the tremble in her hand wasn't obvious.

"Thanks," she said again.

Kaitlyn reached over and rubbed her back. "Do you want to talk about it?"

Aster shook her head. "Actually... please don't mention that to—"

"I won't," Kaitlyn said gently.

Aster sighed with relief. She could tell that Kaitlyn was holding back a dozen more questions.

"I never broke my promise, by the way," Aster said, trying to change the subject. "I never went to any planets."

"Well, you know how I feel about that," Kaitlyn replied, looking at her lap. "But I... shouldn't have made you promise me."

Aster had been so curious about skies and weather and

birds when she was small, and Kaitlyn had elicited the promise multiple times. It wasn't the hardest one to keep—traveling to a planet would have meant a lot more preparation with meds and inoculations and formal clearance. Hopping from one station to another as she felt like it was just the pattern she'd fallen into.

"Also . . . I'm sorry for what I said when you first got back," Kaitlyn said in an unusually small voice. "I shouldn't have unloaded on you like that. I hope you know how glad and relieved I am that you're here and that you're alright. I never meant to sound like—"

"No, Mom," Aster said. "I understand. I'm relieved, too."

Kaitlyn met her gaze with sad eyes. "You do understand, don't you? You've really grown up."

"Finally," she said with a smile.

They both laughed a little, and then Kaitlyn held her arms out in silent invitation. Aster scooted closer and was pulled into a much tighter hug than she expected. All at once, she realized something she hadn't really thought about before: Kaitlyn was a lot like Cori in some ways—both gentle and fiercely protective. She had also been deeply passionate about her work, in helping people relax and feel better. That thought sparked an idea.

"Off-topic question," Aster said as they faced each other again.

"Hmm?"

"How did you decide to start doing massages?"

Kaitlyn looked thoughtful. "It was something I had enjoyed receiving, and I always admired the way the therapists were so calm and comforting... When I got older, I thought that if I could help people *feel good*, more connected to their bodies, that would be rewarding to me."

Aster had heard some of that before. "Was there some kind of certification?"

Kaitlyn gave her a curious look.

Aster shook her head, laughing a little. "I thought of something I might like, but I don't have any experience in it, so I'd be starting at square one. Just wondering about how the process worked in your field."

Her seed of an idea felt too new to share, and her mother was kind enough not to pry.

"Well, yes, I did take courses to get licensed. I had to be recertified every five years before I retired. I took some extra courses, too, so I could learn about new techniques and research. Just to stay fresh. But that was fun for me."

"That makes sense."

"Listen," Kaitlyn said with a smile. "There's no work in the galaxy that's exciting or fun every single day. I know I don't have to tell you that. But if you can find something that speaks to you, that you feel *matters*, it'll be that much easier to stick with."

Aster nodded. "I think I'm on the right track."

Just then, Cori arrived at the open door. "Knock, knock."

"Hi!" Aster stood from the couch to greet her. "So?"

"It went well!" Cori said, looking at each of them. "I'll be working nights to start out, but I figured we could make that work for now."

"Of course we can. Cori, that's great." Aster pulled her wife into a happy embrace, excited to think that everything was falling into place.

20

New Life

Aster was tending to an ivy plant on the edge of a bridge, pulling off dead leaves and watering, when she noticed tiny sprouts peeking through the soil and marveled for a moment. The plants didn't know they were growing in space. They just needed the proper conditions—soil and water and light and care—and they would thrive. As a child, Aster had often taken the greenery on Centauride for granted, having seen it every day of her life. But now, she knew how special it was to live somewhere that maintained lush vegetation all over.

She had also gained a deeper appreciation for the plants themselves, thanks to the botany courses she had completed to become certified for this role. When she started, it felt like a good option for practical reasons—it was work she could do without needing to speak to anyone and it would genuinely benefit the station—but in the months since then, it had developed into a genuine passion. Aster had since found that she never grew tired of expanding her knowledge of plant science, and Cori was always happy to listen to her ramble about whatever she was learning.

The nice contacts Aster had purchased on Ascension were able to sync with the Centauride network as well. After updating the logs to confirm she had completed this section of the zone, she gave her hoverchair a little boost to carry her up over the railing, where she landed her feet on the bridge and shut off the chair, hoisting it to her back with the straps. A kid nearby watched her with wide-eyed wonder. Aster winked before starting on her way home.

Cori had thankfully been moved to the day shift at the clinic, though she was still working part-time. Since she was off work today, she was already in the apartment, and Aster was greeted by the delicious scent of their dinner.

"Hi!" Cori said, turning away from the pot of soup and pulling her into an eager embrace. "How are the plants?"

Aster laughed—that had become her standard greeting. "Excellent. How are you? That smells amazing."

Cori smiled. "Good. I missed you." She pulled Aster to her lips, then, for a long kiss. "I saw you today," Cori added after a moment, pressing another kiss to her jaw. "I was a level down at the market while you were up above on an overpass. I watched you for a while."

Aster laughed again at the mental image. "You must have looked stoned."

Cori shrugged and touched her face. "I'm so proud of you."

It was only about the thousandth time Cori had said so—she had been elated to see Aster take such a liking to the course and even happier to see her throw herself into the work. By contrast, Aster's mothers had expressed polite support when she mentioned the new job, perhaps understandably skeptical that she'd stick with it for very long.

But she hoped lots of things about this new chapter of her life *would* stick.

They moved to the bedroom shortly, Cori pulling her into a tight hug when their clothes were shed. Above her in bed moments later, Cori trailed kisses across Aster's torso, as she often did.

"I love you," Aster breathed, panting, holding her close as Cori rocked against her.

Cori opened her eyes. "I love you, too."

They lay together for a while in the happy afterglow before Cori threw on a robe and went to check on her soup. Soon after, the door chimed, and Aster found her *mother* on the feed from the camera. They both scrambled to get dressed before answering.

"Mona!" Cori said as they greeted her. "What a nice surprise!"

"I'm not really here," she said. "I'm on a secret mission

to find out if you're alright with a little ... *party* at our place for your birthday tomorrow."

Aster laughed and shook her head. She had never been one to make a big deal of her birthday, but it wasn't a shock that her mothers wanted to—especially this time.

"They both wanted to *surprise* you with it, but I just wanted to be sure it's not too much."

"Wait, an actual party? Like with ... *guests*?"

"No, no, just us. But ... well, dinner and cake and all the rest. Kaity wants to hang streamers."

Aster laughed again. "She knows I'm thirty and not ten, right?"

"I keep reminding her."

Aster shook her head again, rubbing her face. She glanced over at Cori, expecting her to be amused by all this, but instead found her looking confused.

"Say the word and I *will* stop this," Mona added. "I'll rescue you."

"No, it's fine," Aster said with a handwave. "Let them do whatever. It's sweet."

Mona smiled. "Thank you." Her expression shifted when she looked over at Cori. "What do you think about a party, dear?"

"Oh, th-that sounds great to me," Cori stammered. "I can't think of a better reason to celebrate."

"That's the spirit!" Mona said. "By the way, my wrists haven't felt this good since I was ten years younger. I painted all afternoon yesterday with no pain. I really can't thank you enough."

"Oh, I'm just glad I was able to help!"

They said their goodbyes, and Mona vanished as quickly as she'd arrived.

After she had gone, Aster turned to Cori, ready to find out the real reason for her silence, but she didn't even need to ask.

"Aster! I am *so* embarrassed!"

"About what?"

"About wh—? All this time we've been together, and I never even *thought* to ask when your birthday was. I know about the tradition, of course, and how important it is, but—"

"Hey, that's okay," Aster said, taken aback. "I didn't mention it, either. It's not like I know when *your* birthday is?"

"I don't *have* one!" Cori said, still exasperated. "We just aged up with each solar year, as a group. There was no special celebration of any kind."

"Oh," Aster said, surprised by her tone. "Are you ... *mad* at me?"

"No," Cori said with a sigh, sounding more like herself. "Of course not. I just regret never asking. I saw your age change in your file on Victory, and I *still* didn't think to notice the date or ask you about it."

"It wasn't a big deal for me. On my last birthday, I ate dumplings in my apartment. It's really just another day."

"Well, *I'm* glad there's going to be a party this time."

They kissed. Aster gave her a playful smile. "Just remember: what goes around comes around."

That expression was clearly new for Cori.

"I *mean* we'll be celebrating *yours*, too," Aster said, speaking over her when she tried to repeat that she didn't have one. "You just said that it's the first of the year. So, that settles it."

Cori laughed. "Okay!"

✳ ✳ ✳

The following evening, as they arrived at Aster's mothers' apartment for the party, Cori maintained a calm facade despite her ridiculous level of excitement. Aster seemed mostly amused, but Cori thought she could see a spark of happy anticipation in her eyes, too.

As Aster's mothers greeted them, Cori looked around. The living room was adorned with colorful garlands and streamers, made out of some sort of shimmery cloth, as well as a HAPPY BIRTHDAY banner and sparkly confetti strewn about the room.

"This is . . . too much," Aster said, taking stock of the decor.

"*Surprise*," Cass said to Aster, a bit pointedly. "You couldn't possibly think we'd do this one halfway."

"It looks great. I do really appreciate it."

Cass turned to grab something and revealed two party hats.

"No," Aster said.

"How cute!" Cori said, taking one and putting it on.

Gathered in the living room, they fell into conversation about years past—about Aster's childhood and her birthday parties back then, and eventually, the day she was born.

"Three decades ago, in this very room," Cass said with a twinkle in her eye.

"Here we go," Aster muttered.

"Really?" Cori asked. "In *this* room?"

Cass nodded and gestured to a section of the floor. "Right here. We had a birthing tub set up for Mona. A nice one with a water heater and a little reclined seat. *I* had the easy job."

"Ah, what was that?" Cori asked.

"I was the errand girl," Cass went on. "Who needs a drink of water? Who needs a hair tie? I was the one running around the house. And then after that, for the main event, I was on left knee duty. Kaity was holding up the right knee—she was breathing even harder than Mona."

Kaitlyn erupted with laughter. "I was *excited!*"

"I thought you were gonna pass out," Cass added, shaking her head.

Kaitlyn laughed again. "I think I almost did!"

"Aw, Kaity," Mona said, patting her knee. "You were wonderful. You stayed with me the whole time."

"Of course I did!" Kaitlyn said fondly, touching Mona's cheek.

The two of them hugged, and Cass looked over at Aster with a triumphant wink. "I've been waiting for this day for a long time," Cass said, speaking to Cori now. "For her to bring someone home so I could torture her by telling this story with an audience."

"Well, she's a *doctor*, so I think she can handle it," Aster said.

"Of course she can, I'm torturing *you!* Oh, one more thing!"

Abruptly, Cass dashed down the hall.

"She's going to get that photo," Kaitlyn said.

"Oh, yeah," Mona agreed.

Aster rubbed her hands over her face. "Cori, brace yourself."

"What am I bracing for?"

"Newborn Aster," Kaitlyn explained. "Minutes old."

Cass returned with a framed photo in her hands. She thrust it into Aster's face first. "Can I show this to her?"

Aster laughed. "Yes, Mom."

The photo placed in Cori's hands a moment later was like nothing she had ever seen before. It showed the four of them, just after Aster's birth: Mona was holding her and visibly emotional, her arms supported by Cass from one side and Kaitlyn on the other. Cass was beaming; Kaitlyn was pressing her brow to Mona's cheek. And tiny baby Aster had discovered her vocal cords.

"Stars above," Cori said, a bit hoarse, feeling Aster slip an arm around her shoulders.

"Cass, you broke her," Mona mock scolded.

"The midwife won a photography award for that shot," Cass added with a hint of pride.

"An *award?*" Aster asked. "Really?"

"Mmhmm."

"I can see why," Cori said.

Aster leaned her head on Cori's shoulder when something beeped in the kitchen.

"Back to work," Cass said, making a quick exit.

"Let me just drop a memory grenade in your evening and then go cook," Kaitlyn mumbled playfully.

"That's Cass," Mona agreed. "Cori, are you alright, dear?"

"Oh yes, I'm excellent. I'm glad she shared that story. And the picture."

✷ ✷ ✷

Dinner was the part of the evening that Aster had genuinely looked forward to. Cass had prepared *two* of her favorite dishes, which made it hard to stop eating before she was bursting—only to remember that there was *cake*, too, and yes, it was also irresistible. Even if its arrival prompted her mothers to *sing* to her, while Cori participated with enthusiastic clapping.

"This was really delicious, thank you," she said afterward, having given in and unbuttoned her pants. "Best birthday in ages."

"One last surprise," Mona said with a sly smile as she passed a small package across the table.

Aster took the box, completely unable to guess what it might be. She opened the lid and found a data chip inside. Mysterious.

"Hmm," she said, tapping her temple to activate her contacts.

Scanning the chip immediately activated a slideshow of nature images: a waterfall. A bird singing in a tree. An ocean—with a cluster of fish jumping out of the water. A sunset. *Your Feronia holiday awaits,* a message read, which then faded to a screen with information that looked like a reservation of some sort—her name, ID, and a confirmation code.

"What *is* this?" she asked, perplexed.

"It's a little trip to the planet Feronia," Mona said. "For you and Cori."

"Oh, wow!" Cori exclaimed. "How fun!"

Aster was still trying to process that. "But . . . that must have been expensive?"

"Nothing we couldn't manage," Cass said.

"We wanted to give you something special," Mona

added. "A belated honeymoon...Plus, we know how you've always wanted to see a planet."

For a moment, Aster couldn't find any more words. Of all the gifts they could have chosen for her, she never would have imagined this—a *vacation* to a *planet*.

She looked at Kaitlyn. "This is okay with you?"

She smiled. "It's a very safe place for tourists. And we know you'll have a *doctor* with you the whole time, so."

All three of her mothers laughed a little. Cori rested her hand on Aster's shoulder.

Aster looked at the reservation again, and her vision swam. "I don't know what to say. Except...thank you."

"We hope you have fun," Mona said. "Happy birthday."

"Take lots of photos," Cass added. "That's required."

"Do you know Feronia, Cori?" Kaitlyn wondered. "It sounds very popular."

Aster was curious about the answer to that question, too.

"Not yet," Cori said, meeting Aster's gaze and smiling. "But I can't *wait* to see it together."

21

Starlight

*C*ori watched as her wife, wearing dark glasses and a sun hat, walked toward her through an outdoor food market in a city called Cybelle on Feronia. It was a bright, breezy day, just warm enough to be cozy in the sun and cool in the shade, which is where Cori was sitting as she awaited Aster's important acquisition of more feronic mountain plums. Thanks to ample sunlight and frequent rain, the fruits on Feronia had a reputation of being exceptionally delicious, and it seemed Aster had already found her favorite.

Taking her seat across from Cori, Aster set down another bowl of fresh yellow slices, triumphant.

"It wasn't just a lucky one," Aster said, taking another bite. "They're *all* that good. Is *starlight* really so different?" Aster was, somewhat stubbornly (and adorably), refusing to adopt the word "sunlight," and Cori wasn't one to insist.

"What do *you* think?" Cori asked, tapping the side of her own sunglasses.

Aster hummed, giving her shades a little nudge down to look out at the scenery with her bare eyes and then recoiling as she shoved them back into place. "Fuck! I think I singed my retinas."

Cori laughed. "It *is* very bright today."

They shared the rest of the fruit. Aster removed her hat, carding her fingers through her hair and reclining in her chair with a sigh.

"How are you?" Cori asked. "Feeling alright?"

It was only their first day on the planet, which meant it was likely that Aster's body hadn't acclimated to the stronger gravity yet—she responded well to the necessary meds before leaving, but there was no way of predicting what would happen planetside. Keeping her fed and hydrated was highly important, so Cori had insisted that they find food before any other activities.

"I'm *fine*," she said with a smile. "I'll tell you if I'm not. You don't have to keep asking."

Cori took her hand. "I'm going to keep asking."

"I know. Should we move on, now?" Aster was eager to see more than just the market, understandably.

"Alright," Cori said. They had rested long enough.

✷ ✷ ✷

Being on a planet was surreal for Aster in many ways, and being there as a *tourist on vacation* felt genuinely absurd. Though her prior travels included many memorable adventures, the point had never been to rest and relax—which was the general vibe on Feronia.

Cybelle was one of a few spaces on the whole world open to human visitors, since the planet was in a protected class due to its robust and delicate ecosystem, and home to no "intelligent" species that would fuck it up. It felt pure, in a way, even if someone did manage to find a way to make it profitable—it was widely marketed as an ideal planet for spacers to visit, both for fun and education. (Coming in on the transport ship from the small orbital station, Aster had seen a school group of spacer children en route to their first planet visit, which had evoked a near-blinding surge of irrational jealousy.)

As Aster walked around the market toward the cliffside, her long hair flapped awkwardly against her neck in the strange wind. There was also a marked difference in temperature from the shade. Aster was literally close enough to a *star* to feel its heat on her skin—so close that Cori had slathered her with special lotion to protect her from *burns*. That fact kept blowing her mind a little.

With the market to her left and the seating area behind them, the view to the right made her the slightest bit dizzy: a vast mountain range, towering rock structures coated mossy green and stretching up to the sky. In the distance, she could see a few white waterfalls, flowing endlessly from impossibly tall cliffs. That land wasn't accessible to visitors and had only been surveyed via drone footage—available for viewing in their hotel room.

"Breathtaking, aren't they?" Cori said beside her.

"Almost like a simulation. Like my eyes don't really believe it."

"I know what you mean."

There was a squawk nearby—they turned to see a large pink bird landing on the shoulder of a young tourist, whose companion was taking a photo. The native bird species, with cute eyes and a puff of yellow on top of their heads, were very accustomed to visitors, and a few more were perched in a tree close by. The goodies in the hotel room included small packs of approved bird food, but Aster was pretty sure they had left it behind—until Cori pulled her backpack around to retrieve a packet, handing it over without even asking.

Aster smiled as she took it, giving her mind-reading wife a look.

"Go on!" Cori said. "I'll take some photos."

The other tourists had moved on now, so Aster stepped closer to the tree and tried tossing a few pellets on the ground. At first, nothing happened, and she wondered if she was doing something wrong, but then there was a flutter of pink, and one of the birds landed in front of her to gobble up the food. She threw a few more; soon, there was a whole feast happening right in front of her. It was funny to think about how the birds must view humans as weird, friendly monkeys who arrived in ships just to bring them treats.

"Hold some in your hand," someone suggested, so Aster tried that next, bracing herself.

Sure enough, one of the flock took interest and flew up to land on her fingers, the little claws of its dinosaur feet poking her skin as it chowed down. Aster stifled a laugh, hoping not to scare it off.

"Perfect!" Cori called out.

The bird flew away as soon as the food was gone, and then Aster noticed a cluster of eager children nearby, flanked by their instructor, who had clearly told them to wait their turn.

"Next!" she said, moving out of the way.

The picture of Aster with the bird on her hand was funnier than she expected. Her mothers would definitely enjoy it. After Cori was situated with her backpack, she pulled Aster into a sudden side-hug and pressed a happy kiss to her cheek, giving her a knowing smile. Aster *may* have admitted that she had dreamed of seeing birds ever since she was a child, and now she sort of wished she had kept that mildly embarrassing information to herself.

"So . . . on to the overlook now?"

"Absolutely!" Cori responded.

They continued on toward the cliffside, joining a small crowd gathered to see the view. Cori had remarked earlier that the breeze "smelled like the ocean"; Aster wasn't quite sure what she was talking about, but now that they were closer and the cool wind was stronger, a particular scent was also much more noticeable.

Not only that, but she could *hear* the water sloshing.

As they made their way up to the viewpoint, she was impatient to get a visual to match the sound—but she was still unprepared for the sight of it.

Directly in front of them, stretching all the way to the horizon, was sparkling blue water. Except for some tall pink rocks jutting out of the water in the distance, there was nothing else for so many miles. Just ocean and sky. The reflection of the sun, rippling on the surface, was both beautiful and blinding, even with her dark glasses.

A large bird passed overhead. It flapped its white wings once and abruptly dove, skimming the water and flying away with a glistening fish caught in its long beak. Multiple observers reacted with awe, but Aster was silent. There wasn't a sound she could make that would properly capture her reaction.

"Look there," Cori said, touching her back with one hand and pointing with the other.

Following her finger, Aster spotted a cluster of sea mammals called mondols, visible above the water for a split second at a time. Even from far away, she could see the sheen of their purple skin and the spouts from their blowholes.

"Wow," was all she managed to say out loud.

Cori embraced her from behind, resting her head on

Aster's shoulder, and Aster covered her hand. As happy as she was to be there, as long as she had waited to see these things in person, something about it also felt bittersweet. Maybe it was the fact that their visit was so fleeting, that she would be back to spacer life soon, and this whole trip would be a memory. Or maybe it was some form of regret that it had taken her so long to see this place, one tiny slice of the abundant, varied life the galaxy had to offer, and there was so much more she hadn't seen, so much more she would *never* experience.

Breaking Aster out of her daze, a uniformed guide offered to take a photo of the two of them. Cori immediately accepted, and they posed together there with the sparkling ocean behind them. When Aster saw the picture moments later, she knew she would never get tired of looking at it.

※ ※ ※

Cori had rarely seen so many blossoms in one place.

They had walked down to the lower level of Cybelle, with its lush natural garden area full of flowers and trees and a stream flowing through the middle. Here, there were landscaped pathways for them to follow, and the salty ocean air was muted under the floral perfume.

Aster was oddly quiet as they went, but Cori figured she was just taking in all the sights. Spotting a large red flower,

Cori stooped to breathe its fragrance and found it incredibly sweet. "Wow. Smell this one!"

Aster copied the gesture, but her experience was less pleasant: she sneezed harder than Cori had ever heard.

"Ugh," Aster said, rubbing her nose. "My whole face itches."

"That's just the pollen. I'll be sure to get you an antihistamine."

"I guess I'm allergic to planets, huh?"

"Well, *most* people are in some capacity. How are you feeling aside from that?"

She shrugged. "I don't know ... A little dizzy."

"Oh? Let's sit for a while, then."

They found a bench nearby. Cori pressed two fingers to Aster's neck, feeling that her pulse was in the normal range. If the meds were to fail, the increased gravity could easily over-exert her heart, like a nonstop cardio workout. But so far, so good.

"I think it's just that there's so much to see," Aster said with a shrug. "Making my head spin."

Cori passed her the water bottle she'd packed.

"Do you feel more at home here?" Aster asked after taking a drink. "Like you're ... back where you belong?"

"Not exactly," Cori said, considering the question. "Certain aspects of it are familiar, but when I was young, I didn't even know places like this existed. How does it feel to you?"

Aster shrugged. "I guess I actually feel pretty out of

place? More than I thought I would. But I'm really glad we're here."

Cori smiled. "Me, too."

✳ ✳ ✳

Later that evening, from the porch balcony of their hotel suite, Aster gazed up at the night sky, full of faint stars. The planet's two bright moons cast ethereal light on the nearby mountains. It had been a while now since the colors of the sunset faded, and she couldn't bring herself to go back inside. She found it comforting to look from here, to remember that technically, everyone was always in space.

The night was cooler and quieter than the day, with no more birdsongs or gabble in the distance. Closing her eyes, she breathed in the air and listened to the trees rustling, wanting to soak in every detail, wanting to commit this place to memory.

Suddenly, Cori was beside her, fresh out of the shower and wearing a fluffy bathrobe. "Look."

She was holding her comm with the weather forecast pulled up—Aster had already checked it prior to their trip, hoping for rain and finding nothing but sunny days ahead.

Cori pointed to a line below the block for the next day, which had been updated to read *Precipitation: 40%*.

"What?" Aster said, grabbing the comm. "Does that mean it *is* going to rain? Tomorrow?"

"It means there's a very good chance. They do their best to predict, but conditions can change."

Aster sighed and nodded, handing back the comm. She really, really wanted to see rain before they left, but she knew not to get her hopes too high.

Cori set the comm aside and slipped her arms around Aster's waist, pressing a kiss to her cheek.

"I hope you get to see it," Cori said. "But if not this time, then someday in the future."

"Really?" Aster asked, blinking. "Like, we could...come back?"

"Of course! Or we could go to *other* planets. Rainy planets. Whatever you want! Now that we know the meds are working fine, I figured you might want to plan future trips."

Aster turned to face her. "You'd really want to travel to lots of planets together?"

"Wh— Of course I would! I'd go *anywhere* with you!"

Laughing, Aster pulled her into a proper kiss, elated to think of this as the first of *many* planetary adventures. With Cori so excited to settle down on Centauride, and this holiday being so expensive and special, Aster had kind of assumed it was a once-in-a-lifetime type of thing that she had to make the most of.

"I like the sound of that," she whispered between kisses, trailing them across Cori's jaw and down to her shoulder, where she pulled the robe loose.

They were swiftly in the plush hotel bed, undressing

with haste. Cori hadn't wanted to do anything *strenuous* when they arrived the night before, so there was some urgency now after waiting.

Making love with the balcony doors open and the night breeze flowing over her bare skin, in gorgeous contrast to the warmth of her wife's body, left Aster feeling ecstatically alive. Nowhere on a station could she feel something like this—like she was reconnecting with a dormant part of her soul.

Afterward, they fell asleep curled up together in the smooth sheets. Aster was deeply grateful to be in such an incredible place with her favorite person. Maybe it was a good thing that it took her this long to get here, so they could experience it together.

✳ ✳ ✳

Cori snapped awake in the early morning. For a fleeting moment, she wasn't sure what had disturbed her, and then she heard a low rumble of thunder—followed by the sound of heavy rainfall.

"Ast—" she started, rolling over and finding that the bed was already empty beside her.

Smiling, she climbed out of bed and found her wife standing on the balcony in a downpour. At first, she waited, letting Aster have the experience alone. The first whisper of sunlight was brightening the sky, muted behind gray storm clouds. But the loss of one pretty sunrise was definitely worth it.

Aster turned and held her arms out in invitation. Cori gladly joined her, instantly drenched as she stepped into her embrace.

"It *does* smell good," Aster said, beaming.

Cori couldn't be sure if Aster was crying or if her face was just wet, but either way, she looked beautiful and precious with her soaked hair and dripping nose and big smile crinkling her eyes. Had she really doubted for one second that Cori would travel anywhere she wanted? That she'd want to live on her home station? That she'd want to be married? Stars above, she'd give Aster anything she asked for. Anything to make her *this* happy.

"Look at you," Cori said, touching her cheek. "How about we go out for an early walk?"

Aster laughed and pulled her into a kiss. "I love you so much."

Cori held her close. "I love you, too."

Acknowledgments

Huge thanks to my dear friend and fellow writer nerd, Amy, for letting me ramble story ideas at her—and for motivating me to grow and improve at every turn. Thanks to the super-talented Jessika for beta-reading and typesetting. A special thanks to my copy editor, Lauren, and proofreader, Elizabeth, for ensuring this story was polished and ready for readers.

Thank you always and forever to my mom, dad, brother, and sister-in-law for your love and support! It means so much. (Extra thanks to my brother for telling me that it "wasn't cringey at all" to order a ring with my main characters' names engraved on it. Extremely validating.)

Thank you to Kate for your words of encouragement and wisdom, to Elyse for always believing in me, to my "brain friend" Rachel for sharing your expertise and answering all my questions (no matter how silly), and to everyone who has never doubted that I had a novel in me.

Thank you to my cat, Chloe, for frequently keeping my lap warm while I write.

And thank *you*, reader, for opening this book and getting this far. I could never express in words how much I appreciate it.

About the Author

Alicia Haberski is a lifelong Texan who discovered a love for stories and storytelling at a young age. For as long as she can remember, she has loved two types of stories more than any other: stories about the distant future and stories where love makes people stronger. She strives to write super-fun sci-fi where queer women get to be brave, fall in love, and have happy endings. At any given moment, Alicia is probably daydreaming about space, wishing it would rain, or chilling with her cat.

aliciahaberski.com
@aliciahaberski

Made in the USA
Monee, IL
03 December 2024